BARELY MISTAKEN
Jennifer LaBrecque

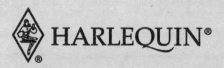

 HARLEQUIN®

TORONTO • NEW YORK • LONDON
AMSTERDAM • PARIS • SYDNEY • HAMBURG
STOCKHOLM • ATHENS • TOKYO • MILAN • MADRID
PRAGUE • WARSAW • BUDAPEST • AUCKLAND

In tribute to all the victims of the September 11th massacre at the World Trade Center, the Pentagon and the empty field in the Pennsylvania countryside. We continue to laugh and love in honor of your memory, which is the greatest refutation of terrorism known to man.

ISBN 0-373-25986-7

BARELY MISTAKEN

Copyright © 2002 by Jennifer LaBrecque.

This edition published by arrangement with Harlequin Books S.A.

Visit us at www.eHarlequin.com

Printed in U.S.A.

_____Prologue_____

OLIVIA SHIFTED on the cold concrete bleacher, and closed her eyes in bliss. Snuggling deeper into a sweater delivered earlier in the week by the church charity group, she absorbed the moment. The bite of a brisk autumn night. The rallying charge of the marching band overlaid by the cheerleaders' chant. The glare of lights illuminating the field in an otherwise dark night. The smell of popcorn, hot dogs, and the occasional waft of hot cocoa. The collective surge of excitement in the stands and on the field.

"Earth to Olivia."

She blinked her eyes open to find her best friend Beth's freckled hand waving in front of her face. "I love football games."

Beth sighed and dreamily eyed the second string quarterback parked on the sidelines. "Yeah. Doesn't Chuck Lamont look cute in his uniform?"

Olivia rolled her eyes and grinned. The question was purely rhetorical. Beth didn't expect an answer.

A frisson of awareness tingled against the back of her neck—the feeling that someone was looking at her. She turned her head. A rowdy group hovered at the edge of the bleachers, drawing several disapproving glares from parents in the booster section. Her gaze skidded to a stop as it locked into the bright blue eyes of Luke Rutledge who stood slightly apart from his crowd. Tough.

Wild. Older. Her stomach flip-flopped and her pulse ran amok, even as a wave of self-consciousness washed over her. He quirked one corner of his mouth in a smile.

If she absolutely didn't know better, she might, for one wild flight of fancy, think one of the sexiest bad boys in the senior class was flirting with her mousy, bookworm self. She attempted to smile back. Her awkwardness produced something much closer to a grimace.

Burning with self-consciousness and an attraction much more intense than the benign crush she'd had on Barry Elwell last year, she glanced away before she made a total fool of herself.

What had seemed like minutes must have only been seconds. Beth remained fixated on second-string Chuck Lamont. Olivia peeked from beneath lowered lashes at Luke. He stood, laughing with his friends, oblivious to her presence. What if some of them had seen her mooning at him? Was that why they were laughing? She shivered into her sweater. *Forget it.* She read too many books and possessed too much imagination.

"So, who wants the scoop?" Amy Murdoch's voice drifted two rows back to Olivia and Beth. Lucy Jacobs and Melissa Bowers, sitting on either side of Amy, squealed their excitement.

Beth screwed up her face, imitating them. "They sound like greased pigs in a race," she muttered to Olivia.

Grateful to concentrate on something other than her imaginary exchange with Luke, Olivia snickered. "Yeah. Kind of." Amy, Lucy and Melissa were the reigning queens of sophomore cool. You only had to ask them.

"Tammy Cooper...health department...birth control pills..." Even though Amy lowered her voice to a conspiratorial level, bits and pieces drifted up to them. Lucy and Melissa visibly gasped.

"...trashy..."

"...in her blood...their mother ran...another man..."

"...Olivia...honor society...same way...born that way."

Olivia blinked hard to stem the tears stinging her eyelids, her flesh crawling with humiliation. It didn't take a rocket scientist to fill in the blanks between the snatches of conversation.

Driven to escape, Olivia surged to her feet.

"Bitches," Beth muttered, eyeing her cup of steaming cocoa and their well-groomed tittering backs with intent. "Meet me in the bathroom. I've got business to take care of."

Olivia stumbled off the bleachers and dashed behind them, desperate to find a dark place to hide. She forced air into her lungs in great shuddering breaths. The words chased around in her head, searing her with their poison. *...born that way...Olivia...same way.* She huddled in the dark, against the cold concrete.

Olivia looked up at a movement. Luke Rutledge stepped into the shadows with her. Olivia's heart hammered. She dashed at the trickle of tears behind her glasses with her gloved fingers.

"Olivia? Are you okay?" His big hands cupped her shoulders. A tremor of recognition rippled through her. She *hadn't* imagined the look they'd shared earlier.

"I'm fine." Her voice squeaked out. She ought to feel threatened. Luke stood six feet tall with broad shoulders and it was dark beneath the bleachers. Instead, he seemed genuinely concerned, almost comforting—totally at odds with his bad boy image.

"You're sure?" He rubbed small circles against her

shoulders with his gloved hands. Even through the layers of gloves, coats and sweaters, his touch left her tingling in a way she'd never felt before.

She shoved her glasses more firmly onto her nose. "Really. I'm okay." Her breath lodged in her throat. She'd never realized how a boy smelled up close. Different than girls. Interesting. Exciting.

"Good." Other girls might've seen it coming, but surprise rooted her to the spot when he pulled her closer and kissed her. She'd dreamed about kisses. She'd read about kisses.

None of it had prepared her for the real thing. His mouth pressed against hers, hot and hard. She leaned into him and kissed him back, giving in to the spontaneous need flashing through her.

...born that way...Olivia...same way. They couldn't be right, could they? But this was exactly how girls from the wrong side of the tracks behaved. Was that why he'd followed her? Kissed her? She was easy? Trashy?

Horrified, she wrenched away from Luke. She ran out of the shadows as fast as her trembling legs carried her.

She was not that way. She wasn't and she'd prove it. To them. To him. And to herself.

1

Thirteen years later...

"YOU'LL BE THE BELLE of the ball tonight," Beth cajoled as she brandished the package of hair color at Olivia.

Olivia paused in the middle of pressing her dress for the costume ball and sprayed extra starch on a pleat that refused to cooperate.

"I'm not concerned with being the belle of the ball," she argued. "I'm quite fond of my mousy brown hair, thank you. Why would I want to trade it in for late-blooming, tramp-in-training red?"

Beth stretched out on Olivia's four-poster Rice-carved bed. "You couldn't look like a tramp-in-training if you tried. Trust me. But you *could* try shucking the prude disguise. You'd be a knockout. A little hair color, some contact lenses and dressing as if you really are twenty-nine instead of sixty-five."

Flamboyant, outgoing Beth just didn't get it. Olivia wasn't interested in being a knockout—not that she even considered herself KO material. Beth was a force of nature. Olivia was a rock. Olivia *liked* her quartz status.

She rolled her eyes at Beth and picked up the long-standing argument. "My eyes are allergic to contacts, as you very well know." She mentally reviewed her wardrobe of conservative skirts and blouses. "And I dress like a twenty-nine-year-old librarian with good taste—"

"Maybe you should borrow something from Tammy."

"Maybe when pigs fly." Her older sister maintained an inverse fashion philosophy—the least amount of clothes showing the most amount of flesh. And Tammy had a bountiful amount of flesh up top. Olivia shook her head as she peered down at her relatively flat chest. "Can you imagine these in one of Tammy's halter tops? Even if I dared to bare, there's nothing there. I'd have enough extra material to make a skirt." Not to mention she'd set every tongue in town wagging.

Beth snickered. "Okay. You've got a point. But at least you'll skip the sag factor. You'll still be Ms. Perky Boobs at sixty when Tammy's playing soccer with hers. Now about this color…"

Olivia pushed her glasses up onto the bridge of her nose and peered across the ironing board at the hair-color model. She'd invested a lot of thought and care into cultivating a conservative, tasteful "look." Olivia always carried with her the sense that everyone in town was watching—waiting for her to slip up, to do or say something inappropriate.

For the span of a heartbeat, a shadow of restless longing tempted her. And then it passed. She shook her head. "Forget it. I'm not going to look tacky or cheap. Adam wants to discuss something important tonight."

The thought brought an involuntary smile to her face. Adam had begun to affect her that way.

"What?" Beth scowled in suspicion.

Beth's scowl dampened her good mood. "I don't know, but it sounded important."

"You've been dating a month, maybe he's gonna put the move on you. Sex is always important to men. Right up there with breathing, eating and television." Beth sighed and placed the hair color box on the nightstand.

"Beth, you've got the gutter mind."

"What's gutter about that? You've been out half a dozen times. He's kissed you, hasn't he?"

"You know he has." Twice to be precise—both times their kiss had proved a pleasant, perfunctory end to their evening. At first, she'd merely considered Adam a friend—a very attractive, very influential friend. Lately, their relationship had taken a more intimate turn. However, it wasn't *that* intimate, yet. "He's mentioned his grandmother's birthday several times. I think he's going to invite me to the party. It seems more likely than sex." Olivia examined the pressed dress. Each pleat lined up in perfect, starched order. "That looks good."

She turned off the iron and hung up her dress. The dark purple complemented her pale skin and dark hair. At least that was the salesclerk's opinion.

"Hmm." Beth cast a considering eye over the floor-length, lady-in-waiting gown. "Almost as stiff and upstanding as Adam. I'm sure he'll approve."

Olivia moved the dress to the back of the door and sat on the opposite end of the bed, crossing her legs at the ankles. Hortense jumped up and settled her immense kitty weight across Olivia's lap. Olivia administered the obligatory scratch behind the ears and turned her attention back to Beth. Usually, Beth was brutally frank—it was one of the things she admired about her long-standing friend—but, for weeks now she'd been beating around the bush, dropping snide comments. "If you don't like him, why don't you just say so?"

"I don't like him."

Hortense seconded the opinion with a short meow.

Ask and ye shall receive. "Why?"

Beth held up a freckled finger. "He's supercilious." She held up another. "He's a snob." A third finger joined the first two. "And he thinks he's all that."

Based on Beth's earlier comments, Olivia had known her friend wasn't wild about Adam, but he didn't deserve this. "That's not fair. He's been a tremendous help in raising money for the new addition to the library. And he's responsible for my invitation to the costume ball at the country club tonight. I should manage to raise another couple of hundred." *And I think he could be The One.* Now wasn't the time to break that particular news.

Beth snapped her fingers. "That's it. You're besotted 'cause he helped you fund-raise. You'd like Freddie Krueger if he helped you with your library."

"You make me sound like the village idiot. It's true, I appreciate Adam's help with the library. Do you know what a difference that new kids' section is going to make—"

"Sure I do, 'cause you've told me." Beth cut her off before she could really wind up on her favorite topic. "Okay, how about this? I caught him admiring his reflection in his office window when I went to make the deposit at the bank yesterday." Beth wrinkled her entire face in disgust.

"So?" Olivia heard the defensive note in her own voice.

"He was so pleased with himself. I bet he got a stiffy."

"What?" Even irrepressible Beth hadn't just uttered what Olivia thought she had. Had she?

Beth tossed her a defiant look. "You heard me, girlfriend. A stiffy. A woody. A boner. Take your pick."

Ewww. She could live without *this* level of bluntness. "If you're going to be disgusting, I'm not listening."

Beth threw up her hands in surrender. "You're warped, Olivia."

Amusement edged out insult. "That's it. My life has reached an all-time low when *you* call *me* warped."

"You're dating the guy, and you think his stiffy is disgusting."

"No. You talking about it is disgusting. He was probably checking his tie or something." Olivia *had* noticed him watching himself in the mirror once when they were out to dinner. "He's very particular about his appearance." She shifted Hortense to a spot on the bed beside her and plucked the new bottle of nail polish off her nightstand. A lifetime of insecurities reared their ugly heads. "I wonder sometimes why he goes out with me."

Olivia began to paint her toenails with meticulous care.

"Are you nuts? You're smart, funny, successful, attractive—in a severely understated kind of way. And you're ten times the person he is."

She paused and raised a brow in Beth's direction. Beth was just a wee bit prone to exaggeration when she climbed on a soapbox. Olivia couldn't resist teasing her. "Ten times? Really?"

Beth scowled at her. "Who was the valedictorian of our graduating class?"

Olivia shrugged and resumed painting her nails. "Who never had a date to the Senior Prom?"

"Who started the local literacy drive?" Beth fired back at her.

"Who was asked out in high school by Deke Richards because he thought her brother could sneak him some beer?"

"Olivia, you've got to move past this 'wrong side of the tracks' label you've given yourself."

"Come on, Beth. My family provides plenty of fodder for the gossip mill. And I didn't have to label myself. My Daughter-of-the-Town-Drunk title was inherited." Along with the faint wash of shame so familiar she wore it like a second skin. Caste systems thrived in small towns.

At times she craved the anonymity and the freedom of living where her background didn't define her. But leaving seemed tantamount to conceding defeat—accepting her title and slinking away in shame. No, she'd vowed long ago to stay and prove a Cooper could contribute more to the community than bail money.

Beth shared a rueful grimace and crossed her

legs Indian style. "Speaking of your family, I heard Marty got hauled in night before last for drunk-and-disorderly."

Olivia sighed in resignation. "Yep. That's my brother, upholding the Cooper family tradition in jail. They even put him in Daddy's old cell. Daddy passed down his spot in the tank." She rolled her eyes. "It does a gal proud."

"And you bailed him out."

"Of course I did. And then I took him home to Darlene and dared her to let him out of the house again." Her sister-in-law had promised to keep her brother, king of the Wild Turkey, home. She shook her head. "Marty's got a good heart and a good mind, when he isn't pickled. But I swear, he spends half of his life drunk and the other half sobering up."

"What about Tammy? Did she really leave Earl for Tim? That girl changes husbands almost as often as I change my underwear."

Olivia shrugged, out of touch with her sister's latest antics. Tammy often made unwise decisions, in Olivia's opinion. Had she left her third husband for his best friend? "I don't know. Likely as not. She wouldn't tell me because she knows I consider that a crazy way to live."

"You, Olivia, are living proof that gene mutation exists. I'd even theorize adoption, but you look like them. Even if you don't act like them. I've never seen one family member so different from the rest."

Olivia's mother swore she'd known her youngest was different from the moment she'd popped out. While she'd named her two other children after country music stars Tammy Wynette and Marty Robbins, her third child didn't seem like a Loretta or Tanya or even Patsy. Hence, she'd named her youngest Olivia, in honor of one of her favorite soap stars. Olivia still clearly recalled her mother spending hours in front of the TV with her soap operas. Of course that was before Martha Rae Watson Cooper abandoned her family in search of greener pastures. Olivia had neither seen nor heard from her mother in twenty-three years.

God knows, Olivia loved the only family she had left—Pops, Marty and Tammy—but they exasperated her. Frustrated her. She'd spent a lifetime trying to rise above her birthright as the white-trash daughter of the town drunk. She often resented the Cooper escapades that were the talk of the town.

Was she so different from them? Every once in a while she gave in to impulse and blew off steam—a skydiving excursion, cold-cocking slimy Bennie Krepps when he tormented a stray cat, attending Willette Tuttle's bachelorette party at a male strip club, a naked midnight dance in a soft summer rain in the privacy of her backyard. If she ever really loosened the tight rein she held herself on, would she make the same poor decisions as the rest of her family?

Maybe she was a shallow person, maybe even a bad person, but the fact that a respected pillar of the community had chosen to date her carried its own brand of validation.

Olivia glanced around her bedroom. Like the rest of her house, it was small, but tastefully furnished. She'd hated the shack she'd grown up in, that her father still lived in. Even as a child, she'd clipped magazine photos of quietly elegant rooms, determined to have a place like that one day, determined to have a life like that one day. Adam, vice president of his family's bank, fit the life she wanted.

She wasn't a social climber. Not by a long shot. It wasn't about fancy cars or diamonds. No, Adam offered the respectability she so craved.

Olivia recapped the nail polish and waved her feet in the air to dry her toenails. "I'm sorry you don't like Adam. We're well-suited."

"Humph." Beth snorted. "If it were me, I'd be barking up the other side of that family tree. Give me Luke over Adam any day. Talk about another genetic curveball. I've never seen two brothers who looked so much alike but were so different."

"No kidding." Olivia suppressed a faint shudder. Luke, the black sheep of the Rutledge family, disquieted her. Worse, he shook her up. Mercifully, he lived in the next county over. He and Adam moved in different circles. And although Luke's company had won the contract for the new library wing, he was out of state, so his partner was heading up the project.

"What've you got against poor Luke? What'd he ever do to you?" Beth turned the tables on her.

Memory of "poor" Luke's kiss from thirteen years ago assaulted her. Had he acted on a dare? A joke? She still had no clue as to why he'd kissed her. All she'd known was that kiss proved true every unkind word she'd overheard between Amy, Lucy and Melissa. She'd run as if Beelzebub himself—actually Luke wasn't far off in her book— had cornered her. She'd never ever mentioned it to anyone. And she wasn't about to confess now. That kiss had haunted her for years. More than once she'd dreamed of Luke and that kiss, only to awaken in the grip of restless discontent.

"Luke's never done anything to me. He's just not my type." A shiver chased down her spine. Damnation. Simply speaking his name set her nerves on edge.

Olivia jumped off the bed and walked over to the dresser, the hardwood floor cool beneath her bare feet. She shifted a stack of mail off her jewelry box and opened it to search for a pair of earrings for the evening. "I can't understand someone born into privilege and opportunity, squandering it by thumbing their nose." She plucked out a pair of amethyst stones in a dangling filigree setting from among the jumble of earrings and held them up.

Beth nodded her approval and went back to the subject of Luke. "Luke's a rebel, all right. I think he was born with a streak of wild in him. The thing about those bad-ass boys, when they finally settle down, they make good husbands. Guess it's 'cause they've sown all those wild oats." Beth shook her head, her eyes dancing with devilment. "And I'd say Luke's almost sown himself out. If I hadn't already invested five years of marriage in Chuck and almost had him trained…"

Olivia laughed, eager to latch on to a topic other than Luke Rutledge. "Yuh-huh. You are such big talk. Chuck is a saint." Well, perhaps Beth's husband wasn't a saint, but he was a very nice man, which was close to one and the same these days. "Not to mention the father of your child."

Beth, nine weeks pregnant, grinned all over herself while she rubbed her tummy. "Well, there is that little matter."

Olivia pulled out the satin-and-lace merry widow she'd mail-ordered on a whim. She unfolded the undergarment and held it up in front of Beth.

"Ooooeeee. Adam is a lucky man." She plucked the sexy lingerie from Olivia and turned it one way and then another. "Hot. Definitely very hot. You go, baby."

"You don't think it's too..." Olivia pursed her lips and pretended to evaluate the underwear "...let's see, how did you describe my wardrobe earlier...oh, yes, prudish?" Actually, she still couldn't quite see herself in such a sexy getup.

"This," Beth dangled the satin and lace from one finger, "is a start. A step in the right direction."

"A start? A step? How about a big flying leap?" Compared to her usual white cotton briefs and the occasional splurge for matching bra and panties, buying this qualified as a veritable walk on the wild side. She felt a little excited and a whole lot naughty just owning such a garment.

"We'll talk flying leaps when you go crotchless." Beth wagged her brows.

"Crotchless?" she squeaked. Olivia imagined herself stretched out on her bed next to Adam, the sheets folded back neatly. In her mind's eye, Adam's expression registered disgust rather than excitement when he noted her crotchless state. "I don't think so. This is plenty wild for me." Olivia toed the line between seductive and trashy, careful not to cross it.

"You've got the right idea in mind. But it seems a shame to waste this on Adam."

Olivia opened her mouth to protest that Adam wouldn't be viewing her underwear.

Beth, who always had to have the last word, laughed and cut her off. "Just kidding. I know you're going to tell me he won't see your underwear."

Her sense of humor surfaced. Olivia smiled a secretive smile, sure to make Beth nuts. Also, just to counteract her predictability.

Worked like a charm. Beth popped off the bed like a spring-loaded action figure. "Are you holding out on me?"

Olivia laughed. "No. It's just a feeling I have."

"It could be gas."

"Maybe it's love." She made a joke of it, in light of Beth's earlier comments. But, just maybe she was on to something. Her feelings had developed into something more than friendship, and Adam had definitely sent similar signals. What kind of husband would he make?

"It's more likely gas. You better go take your shower if you want me to help with the hair and makeup. What time is Adam coming by for you?"

"I'm meeting him at the country club around eight-thirty. I need to check on Pops before I go, and there's no need to drag Adam out there with me."

"Mr. High and Mighty too good to go out to the farm with you?" Beth asked, sniffing.

"No. He's been before. And he was very nice." Perhaps he'd laughed a bit too heartily, his air faintly patronizing, but her father was a far cry from his. Two beers shy of polishing off a twelve-pack, Pops had been feeling no pain as he'd subjected Adam to the farm tour in his rundown pickup. Actually, Adam had requested the tour. Pops maintained, drunk or sober, that it didn't matter how much money was sitting in the bank or buried in the backyard, if a man owned land, he was wealthy beyond compare. Even if the screen door was held together with duct tape. She hadn't invited Adam out again.

"He has a meeting late this afternoon. Something to do with policies regarding special deposits. He may be running a little late to the party."

Beth shoved her toward the bathroom. "So will you, if we don't get you ready. And don't forget to shave your legs!"

LUKE RUTLEDGE PULLED INTO the garage next to the stables and killed the engine. He slid out of the driver's seat and slammed the door. His parents' his-'n'-her matching Cadillacs, his brother's late-model BMW and Luke's old pickup sporting the Rutledge & Klegman Construction logo along with more than a few dings and dents. Which one of these did not belong? He grinned at the joke only he found funny.

A pirate costume hanging in the back of Adam's car caught his eye. His brother as a pirate? He didn't think so. Adam was definitely the starched chinos and tasseled loafers type.

Luke crossed the manicured lawn of River Oaks to the back of the Greek Revival mansion. The return of the prodigal son to his ancestral home. He knew exactly how his father regarded him. The black sheep once again darkening the door.

He'd displayed a knack for finding trouble early on. At what age had he finally figured out that not everyone fell prey to the wildness that seized him at times? He couldn't put an exact memory to the time he realized he was different from the rest of his family. But lines had become clearly drawn about the time he'd discovered they primarily cared about money and position and they figured out he didn't give a damn what people thought.

Rutledges didn't ride big, black motorcycles, sport tattoos, wear an earring, or make a living at something as menial as manual labor. It didn't make a rat's ass difference he'd earned a civil engineering degree, owned his own construction firm, and had more money sitting in the Colther Community Bank than he'd ever need. He'd tainted his success when he'd gone into business with Dave Klegman, a transplanted New Yorker.

Nope. Luke didn't look like a Southern gentleman. He didn't conduct himself like a Southern gentleman. He didn't judge people by their last name or the amount of money they did or didn't have. Luke didn't measure up to Rutledge standards.

He paused at the mudroom that led to the kitchen and checked the thick soles of his scuffed work boots. Ruth would have a piece of him if he tracked mud in on her floors.

The familiar noise from the kitchen brought a smile to his face. *Thunk-rolllll, thunk-rolllll, thunk-rolllll.* Ruth rolling out piecrust. An assortment of smells wafted out on the early evening air, evoking

earlier years as clearly as a photo album. Chicken
and dumplings, blackberry cobbler, crisp pickles,
pungent turnip greens—some of his better boy-
hood memories. Ruth had cooked and run the
house at River Oaks since before he'd been born.

Luke stepped into the kitchen. Ruth paused in
midroll, a smile joining the other creases in her
worn face. "Bless my soul, you're a sight for sore
eyes. We haven't seen you in almost two months."

"Been over in Mississippi on a big job for the last
six weeks. We wrapped it up early."

"Well, it's good to have you home." She shook
her rolling pin in his direction. "Did you check
your boots?"

"Clean as a whistle. And you're still as pretty as
a picture." Luke wrapped an arm as far around her
ample frame as possible and kissed her weathered
cheek. Although her salt-and-pepper hair had lost
its pepper and was a snowy white, Ruth's blue
eyes remained sharp. He glanced at the mountain
of food on the sideboard. "Getting ready for
Grandma Pearl's big birthday bash tomorrow?"

"I've been cooking for three days now." She leveled a stern gaze his way. "You are coming, aren't
you?"

"Would I miss a chance to be held close to the
family bosom? Uncle Jack'll be three sheets to the
wind." Uncle Jack managed to get wasted at every
family function and generally invite disgrace. Luke
liked the old reprobate. He and Uncle Jack shared a
penchant for trouble. "And Grandma'll be thump-
ing her cane and threatening to disinherit everyone. I wouldn't miss it for anything."

His stomach issued a loud growl. "Any chance

of me getting some of those leftover chicken and dumplings?"

"Guess you should've showed up at lunch like decent folk and then you could've had some." Despite her fussing, Ruth spooned up a generous portion.

"Wouldn't want to ruin my reputation by doing anything decent folks might." He accepted a bowl of homemade heaven with a grin. "Actually, I was double-checking the supply list for the library's new addition. Our crew starts work on Monday."

"Olivia's mighty excited. But then she's worked real hard to raise the money." Ruth and Olivia Cooper's father claimed distant kin. Ruth resumed rolling her crusts.

"She must've busted her…butt. It's a nice addition. A new ivory tower for her to lock herself away in her library castle. How is Lady Olivia? It's been years since I've seen her." Olivia. Just speaking her name knotted his gut. He'd known thirteen years ago, she was far too good for him. When she'd pulled away and run from him as if he'd tainted her, he'd vowed to stay away. He could live without that kind of rejection. Especially when so many other girls had been willing. He'd talked to the assistant librarian earlier today, but Olivia, with her solemn gray eyes and touch-me-not air, had been conspicuously absent.

Ruth lowered surprisingly delicate brows in her weathered face. "You'd be a far sight better off with someone like Olivia than those trashy women you're too ashamed to bring home to meet your mama."

Luke shrugged off Ruth's rebuke as he spooned

in a mouthful of dumplings. So, he liked women that ran as fast as his motorcycle. He wasn't ashamed, just never interested or involved enough to bring them home to meet his mother. "I believe your dumplings get better every time I eat them."

"Changing the subject ain't gonna change the fact that you ought to stop chasing tramps."

"Should I chase the fair Olivia?" He laughed but somehow the idea didn't sound as ridiculous as it should have.

"Nope." Ruth plunked the rolling pin down on the counter. "Adam beat you to it. They've been seeing one another." She sniffed in apparent disapproval.

Startled, Luke paused, his spoon in midair, his entire body taut with surprise and a gut full of instinctive protest. "Olivia and Adam?" He wasn't a snob, but his family sure as hell was—it was one of the major differences that formed the chasm separating them. "Dating? When did this happen?"

"A little over a month and a half. Maybe two."

"About the time I headed to Mississippi."

"Um-hmm." Ruth cut out the crusts with practiced economy and draped them over two pie plates mounded high with apples and cinnamon. Her nimble fingers tucked and shaped the pastry. "Can you imagine?"

Luke put the bowl on the counter, his appetite gone. Actually he could and that was the problem. Apparently Olivia hadn't run like hell when respectable Adam kissed her. Thirteen years and her horrified flight from him still rankled. Thirteen years and he still remembered the sweet innocence of her lips, her brief flare of passion. "Can't be very serious. They haven't been seeing each other that long."

Ruth slid the pies into the oven and straightened, sending him a dark look. "How long do you think it takes?"

For what? hovered on the tip of his tongue before he thought better of it. Never mind. It wasn't his business and he really didn't give a damn, even though the idea of Adam and Olivia nettled him, like a splinter beneath his skin.

Luke shoved away from the counter without comment. "I stopped by to see Mother. Any idea where she is?"

"Mrs. Rutledge headed down to the river. She's been painting late in the afternoons. The Colonel's in his study."

They both knew she'd added his father's whereabouts, not so Luke could seek him out, but as a warning. His mother might not understand him, but she loved him fiercely. The same could not be said of his father. "Thanks, Ruth. Great chicken and dumplings, as usual."

"I've never known you to leave more than a bite of 'em in a bowl before." A hint of speculation glimmered in her eyes. "I'll save them for you."

Without comment, Luke let himself out the back door of the kitchen and headed for the path that skirted the terrace and led downhill to the muddy banks of the Cohutta River. He pulled out a thin cheroot and paused beneath the broad arms of a river oak to light it.

"How much longer will you have to see that Cooper girl?" His father's voice carried clearly from the open French doors of his study. Luke stilled the lighter, the unlit cheroot clenched in his teeth. Even though he couldn't see the Colonel, the disdain in his voice clearly painted the sneer on his face.

"Only a little longer. She's an ice princess, but she'll come around. I'll put a ring on her finger if I have to." Adam laughed in derision.

People swore Adam and Luke sounded alike. His own mother often couldn't tell them apart on the phone. Luke hoped he didn't sound like a pompous ass. And he shouldn't be so damn glad to hear Adam refer to Olivia as an ice princess. She might not run in the other direction when Adam kissed her, but it also sounded as if Adam hadn't tapped into the passion Luke knew simmered beneath her surface.

"Good God, I hope it doesn't come to that. But do what you have to do. There's a lot at stake here."

Well, well, well. Adam was dating Olivia because she could help him somehow? Luke rubbed his jaw.

"At the party tonight, I'll invite her to Grand-mother's birthday celebration."

What strings could she pull for a powerful Rutledge? Whatever was going on, it didn't bode well for Olivia.

Luke leaned against the rough bark of the tree and squelched his inkling of protectiveness. Olivia was a big girl. She could take care of herself. Luke was nobody's hero and it'd stay that way. He'd hate to ruin his reputation.

"What about—" The shrill of the phone, his father's private business line, masked the name. "—Will he be there?"

Adam's "Yes" coincided with another ring of the phone.

His father answered, held a brief conversation and hung up. "That was Boswell. You need to meet with his man tonight."

"But what about the party? I've already got a pirate costume and everything." The outfit in the car.

"Forget the party. You can get the final bid information later. Meeting Boswell's man is more important."

Boswell? Had he heard that name before? This was getting more interesting by the minute.

"But that's a three-hour drive. I won't get back here until two in the morning."

"Put a sock in it, son. We're so close now, I can smell the money. Take the farm truck. Your car draws too much attention and you don't want that."

Luke shook his head in disgust. Adam had always been something of a bootlicker, but when had he so thoroughly become his father's puppet?

"Of all the rotten timing. I spent a lot of money on my pirate outfit." Maybe Adam would like some cheese to go with that whine.

"Shut up about your pirate costume. Dress up in the goddamned thing when you get back home," the Colonel snapped. "You've got to leave within the hour. Meet me back here and I'll have the money ready."

Inside, a door opened and closed.

Luke pushed away from the oak and backtracked to the garage. He'd see his mother tomorrow at Grandma Pearl's party. What the hell were his brother and father up to? Walking in and demanding answers would get him nowhere. Who, other than Olivia, had Adam planned to meet tonight at the party and what information did he need? And why would Adam willingly engage himself to a woman he referred to as an "ice princess"?

And what difference did any of it make? He could just walk away and pretend he'd never overheard that particular conversation. He'd head back home. Maybe stop off at Cecil's Bar and Grill and throw some darts.

A full moon waited, heavy and ripe in the eastern sky, even as the sun edged toward the horizon. A familiar restlessness gripped him. He stepped into the cool dark of the garage and flipped on the lights.

Glimmering metal caught his eye. The scabbard housing the sword in Adam's back seat, part of the pirate costume. Is this how pirates felt. Edgy? Restless? Seeking a treasure or excitement? Unsure of what they wanted, but knowing they wanted something? He'd felt this way all of his life. And it usually got him in trouble.

The eyepatch beckoned him. The scabbard flashed her beguiling jewels. The dark wig was about the same length as his own shoulder-length hair. They entreated him, calling to the always-lurking wildness in his soul. A slow smile edged his mouth as an idea took hold.

The car. The costume. The country club. The companion. Opportunity knocked and Luke answered. Could he pull it off? He and Adam sounded alike, and they were about the same build. Luke was darker than Adam, but with low lighting and a costume, if he could figure out who the mystery contact was, he might get some answers. Perhaps a dance or two with Olivia. Then, if he dropped some information her way, it shouldn't be misconstrued as some misguided attempt at chivalry. It would constitute a leveling of the playing field.

Why the hell not? What could be more befitting of a pirate? And what could go wrong in a couple of hours out of one night?

2

"OLIVIA? OLIVIA COOPER? Is that you?"

Olivia forced herself not to squint, although she couldn't see. Against her better judgment, she had surrendered to folly and abandoned her tortoiseshell specs in her car. The ballroom's lighting consisted primarily of candles. She could barely see. Actually, being half blind lent her Dutch courage. She'd mixed and mingled and already raised more money for her beloved library expansion.

The man stepped close enough for her to identify him.

"Hi, Jeff." An ambitious manager at Adam's bank who resembled a rodent, Jeff looked much better as an obscure blur.

"Where's Adam tonight?" he asked, eager for a suck-up opportunity, no doubt.

Blurred vision or not, she still saw Jeff ogling her cleavage. Olivia forced herself not to check herself out as well. Amazing. She actually had cleavage. That merry widow had done impressive things to her small breasts. They not only appeared fuller, they felt fuller as they strained against what had once been a modest neckline. The bra's stiff lace teased her nipples. Further emboldened by a cat's-eye mask and her upswept hair, Olivia felt sexy and terribly provocative. It was a heady sensation.

"Adam? He had a meeting late this afternoon and

thought it might run late." The party was in full swing and still no Adam. She bit back her disappointment.

"When you see him, tell him I'm looking for him." With a final glance at her chest, Jeff took off to suck up to someone else.

Outwardly, she hoped she appeared her usual calm, composed self. Inside she was strung as tight as a crossbow. Good thing she didn't drink, or she'd be tempted to knock back a few shots of Marty's Wild Turkey. Instead, she slipped through a side door and stepped out into the crisp autumn night. The moon, a golden orb swollen with promise, hung suspended above the semi-dressed branches of water oaks and pines.

Olivia steadied herself against the rail of the wrap-around porch. How many times had she listened to other girls chatter about their dates at country club soirees? Now she was one of them. Or she would be once Adam arrived.

As if her thoughts had conjured him up, headlights flashed down the azalea-lined driveway. Olivia recognized the hum of the BMW's engine. A sudden case of nerves had her tucking hairpins more securely and plucking at her mask. What would Adam think of her costume?

She watched as he pulled up and relinquished his car to the club's valet. Her breath caught in her throat, as her pulse pounded.

Wow! Blurred vision or not, there was no denying the pirate outfit tripled Adam's sex appeal. Was it the eye-patch or the Errol Flynn shirt or the wig and tight breeches that lent a sexy swagger to his stride? Something primitive awakened and responded to his saunter. For one brief, disruptive second Luke Rutledge came to mind—doubtless conjured up by Beth's earlier chatter.

She brushed the thought of him away, much as she might a pesky mosquito. Luke was a pompous ass.

Instead she concentrated on Adam.

She gathered her wits as he climbed the broad stairs. "Adam," she called to him, her voice a disgusting squeak. "Adam," she tried again, this time sounding more like herself instead of a mouse on steroids.

After the slightest hesitation, he turned in her direction. "Yes?" His steps slowed as he walked toward her. A tall, dark, mysterious stranger.

"I wondered when you were coming." Her voice came out low and husky.

"Olivia."

How many times had he spoken her name in the past several weeks? Countless. Yet it had never slid off of his tongue like a caress. She didn't need clear vision to feel the heat of his gaze as it flicked over her. He stopped before her.

Adam usually wore a trendy cologne she found somewhat cloying, but tonight he'd abandoned it. His clean, masculine scent, mingled with the sharp, cold, autumn air, aroused her.

Mercurial, quicksilver heat spread through her. Alarmed her. The staid, practical librarian demanded retreat. She stepped back and the darkness engulfed her. The distance didn't diffuse the awareness that shimmered and danced between them.

Adam followed her into the shadows, the broad expanse of his shoulders silhouetted against the moon. "You're beautiful. You take my breath away, Lady Olivia."

Oh my. She checked the urge to make sure he wasn't talking to someone else and decided to try something new—gracious acceptance. "Thank you."

"We should go inside. It's cold out here."

His low-timbered voice shivered against her skin. His words said one thing, his body language said something else as he dipped his head toward her.

"Yes. We should..." Instead, she stepped closer, drawn to him regardless of her will.

"...go inside." Even as he finished her sentence, he cupped her shoulders and drew her forward.

She braced her hands against the smooth texture of his shirt, the spring of male hair beneath tantalizing. Evocative. Unnerving. "Tell me why again," she murmured.

"It's cold."

Every inch of her body responded to him. The black velvet mask pressed sensually against her face while the night air's cool fingers brushed against her heated skin. "Is it?"

She'd accepted Adam's kisses before. Now, for the first time, she *craved* his kiss.

"Olivia?"

Her insides melted at the rich roll of her name on his lips—an auditory aphrodisiac. The night and her vision—or lack of—blurred reality, yet intensified her other senses. The steady rhythm of his breathing whispered a melody to the background accompaniment of the party's muted sounds. His scent evoked an awareness deep within her.

Her breath mingled with his. As inevitable as the rise of the moon or the rustle of the wind through the dry leaves, her lips welcomed his.

And her world turned upside down.

Passion, long dormant and unacknowledged, awakened with an almost frightening intensity. Had she ever felt this way before? A ghost of a memory danced in her head, but wrapped in the feel and taste of him, Olivia gave it no credence.

Was it the full moon? Maybe the mask? Or simply because it felt so undeniably good? She didn't stop to delve into motives. Instead, uncharacteristically, she abandoned herself to the situation and the sensations flooding her. She leaned into him and deepened their kiss.

Thus far in their relationship, Adam hadn't been very physical. On the odd occasion when he was, his touch verged on platonic. Although he'd hesitated for the briefest moment, there was nothing platonic in the way he slanted his mouth over hers.

Olivia grasped his shoulders more firmly, as much to support herself as to enjoy the play of hard muscles beneath her hands. She silently apologized to Adam for previously thinking him a bit on the soft side. He was deliciously muscular and firm.

And his kissing had come a long way since the last time. They both came up for air. Olivia slumped against the brick wall for support. Adam braced himself against the same wall, his hands on either side of her. How was she supposed to catch her breath and recover from that kiss with his breath warming her face, his body mere inches from hers?

A few feet away, a window scraped open. Laughter and music spilled onto the porch, shattering their cocoon of intimacy. "It's hot in here," a woman's complaint drifted out.

Olivia corrected her posture and Adam straightened, dropping his arms to his sides.

"We should go inside. It sounds as if it's much warmer in there," Olivia regained her voice along with her coherence.

Together they moved toward the door. Adam's fingers found the small of her back and settled there. Shivers chased along her spine.

"It can't be any hotter than it is now." Adam's muttered comment absolutely wrecked her small measure of composure as they joined the party.

LUKE NAVIGATED through the crush of people hovering about the door without stopping to talk. Kissing Olivia had damn near rendered him incapable of speech. He was still reeling from the impact of that kiss. Holding her in his arms, tasting her mouth, breathing in her scent, had felt like a homecoming. Thirteen long years and he realized the way he'd felt during that first kiss hadn't been a fluke. He barely refrained from grinning like an idiot. If Adam had ever experienced even a sampling of Olivia's brimming sensuality and passion, he'd have never referred to her as an ice princess.

He mentally compared the country club to Cecil's Bar and Grill. As a matter of course, Luke didn't frequent the country club. This was foreign territory. No dartboards. No pool tables. No neon lights advertising beer. No babes in leather bustiers.

Just as he'd anticipated, the lighting in the ballroom consisted of candles on small, white-clothed tables scattered around the dance floor perimeter. A cash bar in one corner did a steady business. He headed the other way. The less contact he had with people, the less likely he was to blow his disguise. Whoever was supposed to make contact with Adam, would surely seek him out. The safest way to avoid conversation was to hit the dance floor, Luke reasoned as he steered Olivia in that direction. And quite frankly, the prospect of holding her close didn't pose a hardship.

The microphone hummed as the song ended and the

band's singer stepped up. "We're going to slow it down before we take a break."

The music began and Olivia turned into his arms with a quiet smile that slammed his heart against his ribs. Unfortunately, her smile was intended for his brother.

"I know you don't like to dance, but I'm glad we're out here," she murmured as he clasped her hand, small and delicate, against his chest. She cupped his shoulder with her other hand. He didn't dance much and certainly not with women like Olivia. She felt amazingly right in his embrace.

He was far happier to know Adam had never held her like this than he should've been.

"You inspire me." He pulled her a fraction closer, achingly aware of her soft curves beneath the stiff starch of her dress. She radiated classy elegance. She'd been too good for him years ago when he'd stolen a kiss. She was still out of his league.

Behind the black velvet mask trimmed in feathers, her gray eyes studied him intently, almost squinting. Did she recognize he wasn't Adam? *No.* He wanted to continue to hold her in his arms and sway to the sultry song. "What is it?"

Tugging her hand free of his, she reached up and rubbed the pad of her thumb against the edge of his upper lip. "I branded you with my lipstick."

To hell with the lipstick, her touch branded him. Her hands drifted farther up, resting between his shoulders and his neck, touching his bare flesh. He'd seen fine-looking women naked and not been nearly as turned on as he was now.

Luke traced his finger along the satin skin near her lips.

"Am I smeared?" Her voice resonated low and husky, her breath warm and moist against his finger.

She wasn't, but it offered a good excuse to touch her mouth. He lingered, tempted by the fullness of her lips and the memory of their recent kiss. "No, they're perfect."

Behind her mask, her gray eyes flirted, as she tilted her head coquettishly. "My Lord Pirate, your flattery goes to my head." Her fingers cupped the nape of his neck. His belly clenched in response.

"And your nearness goes to mine, Lady Olivia." Both of his heads.

With a sigh, she melted against him. *This* was the woman his brother referred to as the "ice princess"? Once again, he was fiercely glad Adam seemed oblivious to the passion that simmered just below her surface, that lit the seductive light in her eyes.

Silently swaying to the music, Luke absorbed Olivia. Her sensual mouth so at odds with the angular lines of her face. The graceful length of her neck that begged to be nibbled. The alabaster mounds of her breasts teasing at her neckline. The curve of her waist beneath his hand. The errant brush of her nipples against his chest. Her subtle fragrance wove about him, tantalizing and exotic. She was a hidden treasure and he knew just the pirate to explore her.

A giant marshmallow dancing with a peanut M&M's bumped into him, jostling Olivia enough to bring her head up off his shoulder.

"Sorry, Adam. Olivia," the marshmallow stammered an apology.

Luke managed not to glare at Mr. Sta-Puf as he steered in the opposite direction. For a few, brief minutes he'd forgotten Olivia was only in his arms on sufferance.

"I forgot to tell you earlier, Jeff was looking for you." The feathers trimming her mask tickled against his chin. Fine strands of her hair brushed his cheek like dark silk.

"Good old Jeff." Who the hell was Jeff? Obviously someone he should know, so he could hardly ask Olivia to point him out. Was he Adam's contact at the party?

The song ended. Couples drifted off the crowded floor as the band dispersed for a break. He twined his fingers through Olivia's, reluctant to release her.

A smile turned up the corners of her mouth and lit her eyes. "I have a table in the back."

Several people greeted them. Luke returned the greeting, but continued to wind his way to the back of the room. Olivia glanced at him in surprise. "You don't want to stop and talk?"

Oh, yeah. Adam was a schmoozer. "Not tonight."

"Here it is." Olivia stopped by one of the draped tables in a back corner. As Luke pulled out a chair for her, she sat in the one next to it. "You can have the seat facing the mirror."

Luke glanced over at a mirror reflecting his pirate image. He bit back a smirk as he sat down. When they were teenagers, he'd teased Adam about frequently checking his appearance in the mirror. Apparently Adam still liked to admire himself. And apparently Olivia had noticed. His knee brushed against hers as he settled his legs beneath the table. The brief contact sizzled through him.

Olivia felt it too. Awareness echoed in her sharp intake of breath and the widening of her eyes. "I raised more money for the library addition tonight," she said in a rush, as if desperate to say something.

"Good. Are you excited construction starts Monday?"

Driven to touch her, he captured one of her hands and brought it to his mouth. He nuzzled the soft center of her palm. Her fingertips curled against his jaw. Her luscious lips parted. She appeared slightly dazed as she murmured a yes.

"You know Luke's going to supervise the job personally."

Her mouth tightened and her hand clenched within his grasp. "But Mr. Klegman is supposed to."

Yes, Dave was supposed to until about two seconds ago when Luke decided he would take on the project. Dave wouldn't care. "Change of plans, I guess."

Olivia tensed. "No one mentioned it to me."

Luke shrugged with feigned carelessness. He knew he shouldn't tread where he was about to go, but daring had always faced down judiciousness. He leaned close, fascinated by the delicate shell of her ear. Luke inhaled her scent with each breath. "Don't you like my brother?"

"No." Her gut response rang low and vehement. She scrambled to recover as politeness warred with truth in the depth of her eyes. "I mean yes. Of course I do."

It was ridiculous that something he already knew carried a sting. It was the why of the matter he didn't understand. Tomorrow—when she realized he'd tricked her—tomorrow she'd have a reason to dislike him, but why now?

"I think your first answer was the truth. Why don't you like Luke, Olivia?"

Her chin jutted at an obstinate angle. She gazed at the flickering candle. "He makes me uncomfortable. He doesn't follow the rules. He's a loose cannon and I've got enough of those in my own family." She shifted her attention to stare directly into his eyes—well, his eye and the eyepatch covering the other one. "I don't want to discuss Luke anymore."

Quite frankly, he'd lost his appetite for hearing why she disliked him. "Fair enough. Why don't I get us a drink?"

"Tonic with lime would be great."

He found himself oddly reluctant to leave her for even the brief time required to fetch drinks. Without forethought or planning, he leaned forward and brushed the soft fullness of her mouth with the hard line of his own. It was difficult to say who was more surprised, her or him. "I'll be right back."

"I'll be here." She appeared as bemused as he felt.

Luke managed to cross the room to the bar without getting snagged into a conversation, which was a good thing because quiet, demure Olivia had thrown him for a loop. Quiet, demure women should have a calming effect on a man. Olivia affected him just the opposite. Something about her stirred up the wildness in his soul. Every damn time he was around her, he wound up kissing her.

He ordered two tonics with lime—as much as he'd like a healthy splash of gin to doctor his up, he needed to keep a clear head and that was already something of a challenge with Olivia. Drinks in hand, he turned and found himself face-to-face with Henrietta Williams, head of the Welcome Committee and a member of the Chamber of Commerce.

"Hello, Adam. You look so dashing as a pirate. I declare, you almost take my breath away." Henrietta batted her lashes and simpered.

It was far more likely that Henrietta's girdle rendered her breathless. Luke, however, in a rare moment of gallantry, refrained from making that observation. "Why thank you, Henrietta. That's quite a..." he searched frantically for a way to describe a woman with the proportions of a sumo wrestler wearing a Geisha getup "um...inventive outfit you have there."

"Candy and I are Oriental sugar and spice tonight." Henrietta giggled behind a lacquered fan, and indicated her daughter at a nearby table. Candy, a younger replica of her mother, both in build and costume, waved in his direction. "I know you're glad to have all that fundraising over with. It was generous of you to give up so much of your time to that Cooper girl. Very sweet of you to invite her tonight to the club." She lowered her voice and raised her penciled eyebrows. "Let's just hope she doesn't get any ideas she belongs here."

"I know what you mean, Olivia's much too good to belong here," Luke even managed to smile at the snobbish battle-ax.

Luke turned on his heel and walked away even as Henrietta tittered behind him. "Now Candy's going to save you a dance as long as you don't make her walk the plank. I'll tell her to look for you when the band starts up again," she sang out to his retreating back.

He cut across the empty dance floor, eager to avoid any more matchmaking mammas.

Luke presented Olivia with the watered-down drink, the ice having given up the fight with the crowded, overheated room.

"Sorry, the ice is pretty much gone. Henrietta Williams waylaid me."

"Let me guess, Henrietta was trying to set you up with Candy." She took the drink. He watched as Olivia tipped the glass, fascinated by the movement of her throat as she swallowed. Moisture dripped from the glass to the valley created by her cleavage. She lowered the tumbler and sighed with satisfaction. "At least it's wet." She held the glass against her neck. "Are you as hot as I am?"

The lack of guile in her gray eyes combined with her sexy words left him dry-mouthed with want. He fought the urge to lick off the moisture where it clung to a tempting expanse of her neck, to follow that wet rivulet to her valley. If she ever realized her own sensuality, she'd be lethal.

"I don't know if I've ever been hotter." Desperate, he tossed back a portion of water, mourning his decision to forego a stiff measure of gin. Alcohol couldn't possibly unhinge him any further.

"Let's take a moonlight stroll in the gardens."

Once again, desire slammed him. "I don't think that will cool us off."

"I know."

A rush of tenderness filled him at the hint of uncertainty flickering in her eyes, despite the invitation issued by her smile. Luke sat rooted to the spot, momentarily incapable of moving, overwhelmed by his good luck.

The microphone squealed as the band's singer announced the next set. In the mirror, he caught a glimpse of Henrietta urging Candy in his direction. That was enough to dispel his inertia.

As the other couples rushed to the dance floor, he slipped out the back door with Olivia.

3

Moonlight danced through bare branches, casting an ethereal spell along the garden path. Gravel crunched underfoot as they passed a fountain where a stone maiden spilled water into a pool below. The fecund fragrance of fertile soil underlaid the brisk bite of autumn air.

Caught up in sensual enchantment, Olivia wouldn't have been surprised to spot a satyr in fleeting pursuit of a nymph. She herself had become a lady-in-waiting absconding with a dangerous pirate. Tomorrow she'd go back to plain Olivia the librarian, but this magical night had transformed her into Lady Olivia.

Neither spoke until they reached a trellised archway where countless couples had exchanged vows over the years. Within the shadowed confines of the archway, Adam turned to her. He wrapped his hands around the back of her neck, tugging her closer with a tender urgency. She'd never guessed such an innocuous spot could be so rich in sensory nerves. She felt his touch all the way to her toes.

Even as she slid her hands around his waist and met his lips with her own, Olivia realized she'd never felt more alive than at this moment. Her eyes drifted closed. His mouth tasted faintly of lime. Was it seconds or hours that they stood wrapped in one another? Olivia had no idea, she only knew it hadn't been long enough when the kiss ended. She leaned back against the latticed wall of the trellis, seeking support. Give Adam a pirate costume and he became a different man.

Adam leaned down and rested his forehead against hers. Just that simple contact and his proximity, and her knees threatened to buckle. It was as if some magic thread bound them together.

"Olivia, I need to tell you something—"

She quieted him with a finger against his lips. "Shh. Tonight's magic." She traced the firm line of his mouth with her fingertip and felt his shuddered response. A thrill shot through her that she affected him as deeply as he affected her. And much like a tiny piece of rich, dark chocolate melting against her tongue, his kisses were sinfully delicious but gone so quickly, she merely craved more.

"But, I'm—"

"Please." She leaned against him and teased her tongue against his lips. "When you…when I…I've never felt that way before when we kissed." Olivia summoned all her courage. "I don't want to talk, I just want to feel like that again."

With a groan, he swooped down and captured her mouth. Forget feeling *that* way again—*this* was even better. His lips probed, fierce yet tender. She opened her mouth to him, eager for the thrust of his tongue against hers. Heat scorched her, from the inside out. He splayed his broad hands against her back to pull her closer, and she arched into him. Her breasts welcomed the hard wall of his chest. She moaned her pleasure into his mouth and felt him swell, hard and fast, against her belly.

A sense of destiny shook her.

He dragged his mouth away from hers. Their

breathing rasped into the quiet of the garden. Before she could protest his abandonment, he scattered kisses along her jawline. Olivia dropped her head back to allow him fuller access to her neck. Quick study, her pirate. As he lavished her with kisses, his breath warm and moist against the chill of her exposed skin, she quivered and her body tightened.

He slid her dress off of one shoulder, baring it to his mouth. "So...very...very...sweet." Nibbles punctuated his words and drove her further out of her mind, into a state of blissful sensation. "So...beautiful." His tongue swirled against the exposed slope of her breast. Desire flashed through her, like a rampaging river swollen by torrential rains.

He slipped his thumb inside her bodice and brushed against her pearled tip. Olivia whimpered. A faint scrape of his thumbnail against her nipple and her hips undulated against him in supplication. He pushed aside the starched material and freed her breast to the nip of the night air.

She felt vulnerable. She also experienced a peculiar sense of belonging and shelter in his arms. Exposed, yet safe. It was an intoxicating combination.

"You..." he cupped her breast in his hand "...are..." he bent forward until his breath warmed her tight bud "...mine?" Part declaration, part question.

"Yes." Part answer, part demand.

He suckled her deep into his mouth, then released her to tug at her nipple with his lips. Pleasure pulsed from her breast to her thighs. She clutched at the lattice behind her, bruising the delicate vine twining around it, and whimpered.

The sharp sound of crunching gravel nearby interrupted. Teasing laughter floated over the flowers and shrubs, as another couple sought the enchantment of a garden stroll.

Olivia froze, acutely aware of her semidressed state in the shadow of the trellis. Before she summoned the wherewithal, Adam restored her clothing with unsteady hands.

Instead of anticipated embarrassment, mild annoyance at the interruption stirred in her breast—and other parts farther south.

The night air carried a woman's voice. "It's cold out here. Let's go back to your house." A man murmured indistinctly, but retreating footsteps left Olivia and Adam alone once again.

Olivia had no intention of squandering even a minute of this night out of time. She smoothed her palms over the flat plane of his belly up to his chest. Standing on tiptoe, she whispered into his ear, "I don't think it's cold at all. In fact, I think it's very, very hot."

His wig, gathered at his nape with a leather strap in true pirate fashion, tickled against her nose, surprisingly silky and real. Tonight Adam had abandoned his hair gel with the annoying odor. She infinitely preferred the clean scent of sandalwood present beneath the wig.

"Honey, you are killing me." His low murmur stirred her hair and her feminine self-esteem.

"Am I really?" Go figure. She, Olivia Cooper, a femme fatale? From the time she'd donned her costume and mask, it was as if she'd slid through the rabbit hole—Olivia in Sensual Wonderland.

He brushed his groin against her, the thick ridge of his erection apparent. "Really."

Her thighs quivered and clenched in response. "Oh, my. Is that a sword in your pocket or are you just glad to see me, Captain Hook?" And now she was glib and flirtatious. Really, altogether *too* strange.

She sensed his smile in the dark as his thumb played against the hollow of her cheek. "Baby, I'm so glad to see you, there's no damn way I can go inside now."

Up until now Adam had always addressed her in a formal manner. His earthy sensuality struck a chord within her.

Where such boldness came from she would always wonder, but she reached between them and palmed him. He pulsed at her touch. "We could go to my house."

"Are you propositioning me, Olivia?" Was that a hopeful note underlaying his incredulity?

She knew she'd stepped—make that leaped—beyond her self-imposed boundaries. But one night. For one night her mask and the shadows offered a measure of anonymity. She drew a fortifying breath and seized the opportunity. "Yes. I believe I am."

"Thank God." He wrapped her in his arms. "Pillage and plunder?"

"Hmmm." Instinct took over. She licked at the base of his throat. He shuddered in response.

"Let's go." The strain in his voice and the fact she'd put it there, excited her.

She traced her tongue against the pulse hammering in his neck. He groaned and set her from him. "Let's go now. No more of that."

Compelled to seek one more touch, Olivia kissed the strong column of his throat. The slight chafing of his beard aroused her unbearably.

"Olivia, you've got to stop." His voice echoed his harsh breathing. "We're about one kiss away from the point when I won't care if fifty people are inside that building. Before I prop you against the lattice, raise your skirts, and slip inside you while you wrap your legs around me."

His words inflamed her. Moisture slicked her. Her nipples further tightened to hard points of want. She teetered dangerously close to the edge of not caring herself. The ten-minute car trip to her house loomed like an eternity.

She couldn't get him home fast enough. "Let's go. You can follow me."

He twined his fingers through hers and tugged her along, leaving the privacy of their hidden corner behind. She sensed his urgent need matched hers. As they reached the front steps of the club, Adam tossed his ticket at the snoozing teenager on valet duty. "I'll be back in a minute for my car."

The boy scrambled for the appropriate key. "Yes, sir, Mr. Rutledge."

Without speaking, they wound through the parking lot. When they reached her car, Adam caught her up in his arms and kissed her hard, as if he hadn't touched her for days instead of a matter of minutes. His mouth's demanding hunger reduced the world to just the two of them. Still holding her in his arms, he raised his head.

"Olivia, I want you to know there hasn't been anyone for a long time."

"Does that mean you're desperate?" she blurted out, her insecurities running away with her mouth.

He chuckled as he slid the backs of his fingers against her cheek. Although she couldn't see it, she felt the intensity of his gaze. "No. It means I'm choosy. Very, very choosy." He bent his head and kissed her, a slow, lip-clinging, mind-drugging, heat-infusing kiss. "But I am desperate for you." He brushed her lips with his once more. "I'll be right behind you," he promised, looking back as he strode away.

Olivia remained against her car, uncertain she was actually capable of driving.

She opened the door and fell into the seat, the bright light of the interior harsh compared to the soft moonlight. Olivia killed the dome light and fumbled for her glasses. She slid her mask to her forehead and donned her glasses. She cranked the car and pulled out of the space. Adam's car lights flashed in her rearview as she turned left onto the highway.

If she hadn't seen him drive up in his car, wearing the costume he'd described earlier, she wouldn't have known him. Tonight everything about him—his voice, his scent, his touch—tapped something deep inside her.

Although she had her occasional wild impulses, there had never been anything of this magnitude. Tonight was so out of character for her, she should be frightened. But it was excitement that rendered her hands unsteady on the wheel. The only thing that scared her now was that Adam might change his mind on the drive.

She checked her rearview mirror. Yeow! Let him get a look at this and he'd change his mind for sure. Tortoiseshell glasses and a black velvet mask hiked to her forehead—not pretty. Without her glasses, she was a one-woman wreck waiting to happen. But the minute she pulled into the driveway, they were history.

LUKE FOLLOWED OLIVIA. *Don't change your mind*, he silently willed her.

But what kind of son-of-a-bitch considered sleeping with his brother's girlfriend? A worrisome remnant of his conscience niggled him. The kind who knew Adam didn't really care about Olivia. The kind who *knew* she had never responded to Adam the way she responded to him. The kind who couldn't manage a coherent thought after kissing her. The kind pulling into her driveway behind her...

In three quick strides he caught up with her as she fumbled with the key in the front door lock.

"Let me help you with that." He reached around her, fitting his hand over hers, and inserted the key. Wisps of her hair tickled his chin. The curve of her buttock teased his erection. His hand shook so badly, it took both of them to open the door. Olivia in her seductive mode stirred the wildness in him to fever pitch.

He followed her into a small, dark foyer. The door barely closed behind them before she turned to him. He reached for her as she launched herself at him, her mouth demanding, her hands eager as they worked at the buttons of his shirt. His body surged a response, impatient to find release in her. He struggled to remember something important he should discuss with her. Her hips ground against him and his brain skipped to autopilot.

Harsh breathing—his—echoed in his ears. She mewled deep in her throat as his tongue parried with hers. He damn near came.

"Honey, we've got to find your bedroom or your couch because I can't—"

"No."

She'd changed her mind. He tensed, painfully near the point of no return. But if Olivia said no, then it was no. "No?"

"Forget the couch or the bed. Here. Now." Her voice, low and husky, seduced him. She stroked him through his breeches, her touch a trail of fire. "Against the wall.

Just the way you described it at the club, in the garden...."

He backed her against the door before she finished her sentence. "Against the wall like this?"

Her sharp intake of breath transmitted her approval. Her breathing rasped as harshly as his own. "Yes."

She unzipped his pants and he sprang free. Luke gritted his teeth and barely held himself in check when her fingers found the thick fluid at his tip and spread it down his shaft.

He jerked up the stiff material of her skirt until it bunched around her waist. He held it in place with one hand. Her breath came in short, sharp pants. Her eyes glittered behind her mask as she brought her fingers to her mouth and tasted him. He could barely speak. "Raise your skirt like this?"

She licked her lips and surged against him. "Yes. Just like that."

He delved between her thighs and discovered wet satin. Pushing the material aside, his fingers found her honey-drenched folds. "Oh, baby." His voice shook. "Put your hands on my shoulders." Cupping the soft, plump mounds of her buttocks, he lifted her and tested himself against her slick wetness. "Liv, you are so hot. So wet."

She wrapped her legs around his waist and strained against him. "Yes. Yes. For you."

For him. *His* Lady Olivia. He lowered her onto his shaft. "Slip into you like this?" He braced her against the door and clenched his teeth. As he slid farther into her, she took him to a place he'd never been before, where the current of emotion ran as fast and deep and twice as treacherous as mere physical desire.

Deep within her body, her muscles tightened around him in response. "Yes. Just like that."

He thrust three more times and Olivia began to climax. The shudder that gripped her, affected him as well. Luke threw back his head and joined her in a release. And for the first time in his life, it was more than a physical release. The fact that they'd just had hard, fast sex didn't diminish the wellspring of jumbled emotion he felt for Olivia.

Her legs still wrapped around him, she slumped against the door. A satisfied smile curved her lips. Male pride surged through him. He had put that smile on her face. And regardless of how fast she ran this time, he'd be right behind her. And doubtless, she'd run. She wouldn't be pleased when she discovered his true identity. But *he'd* discovered the buried treasure and he wasn't giving her up. She was his booty.

She opened her eyes with a flutter of lashes. A subtle shift of her lips transformed her smile to suggestive seduction. She trailed her finger down his chest to his belly and beyond to where their bodies remained joined. "Ready for a little pillage and plunder?"

OLIVIA TUMBLED back onto her bed, bringing Adam along with her. For the first time ever, she wished she owned something more risqué than pima cotton sheets. For the first time ever, she'd discovered delicious satisfaction and the restless ache for more.

Moonlight filtered through the sheer drapes at the window, bathing the room in a soft glow. It reinforced the surreal quality of the night. She'd swear she'd embarked on an out-of-body experience, except her body was very much involved. The red blink of the answering machine on her bedside table heralded a message. A responsible woman would check her messages. But she'd thrown off that particular gown tonight. Quite frankly, she was much more interested in her pirate than finding out if Marty had landed himself in jail or if the literacy council was meeting next week. She ignored the persistent blink of the red light.

"I'm sure you'd be much more comfortable out of that dress," Adam teased as he reached behind her and tugged at her zipper. In the amount of time she'd known him, he'd never teased before. She liked this playful side of him. But then again, he'd done a lot of things tonight he'd never done before. And she liked all of them. She could get used to him sprawled across her bed, coaxing her out of her clothes.

Olivia slid off the bed and shimmied free of her starched pleats. She'd lost her earlier sense of urgency, yet not the anticipation of touching him again. Slowly, she raised her hands to the pins in her hair, conscious of the upthrust of her breasts. With sensual deliberation, she released her hair, exhilarating in the weight and slide of it against her bare shoulders. She stood, clad in her mask and merry widow, illuminated by moonbeams.

From the shadows on the bed, Adam sucked in a harsh breath. Excitement coursed through her. She had never associated sex with power. It had always meant a measure of subjugation. But now there was a subtle shift of power back and forth between she and Adam and subjugation wasn't an issue.

She knelt on the bed and crawled forward on all fours.

"Olivia." He rasped her name even as she moved between his thighs and up his body. She stretched out next to him on the bed.

"I'm sure you'd be much more comfortable out of

those clothes." She tossed his words back at him. It was her turn to watch him. She squinted in his direction. Or as close as she could come to watching. *Now* struck her as a bad time to grab her spare glasses off the nightstand.

Actually, it was terribly arousing to rely more on her sense of smell, taste and touch. The scent of satiation perfumed the air between them. She ran her tongue over her lips, enjoying the taste of him, hungry for more.

Adam got rid of his clothes in record time. She couldn't see, but she discerned his general outline. Broad shoulders, flat belly, powerful thighs, and...*oh, my.* Her various body parts quivered and shivered and generally transmitted their approval of him naked.

And then he was back beside her, solid and warm and so overwhelmingly male her breath caught in her throat. He buried his hand in her hair, his fingers massaging her scalp. She wrapped her arms around his muscular neck. A kiss. She wanted one desperately.

"Olivia, I'm not—"

And *women* wanted to talk things to death? She kissed him. Okay, maybe more along the lines of attacked. Catching him in midsentence, she slid her tongue into his mouth. Men generally didn't do well with multitasking. She wagered he couldn't kiss and think at the same time.

With a muffled groan, he answered her call to action, his lips as demanding as hers. She strained against him, burning with a fever only he could cure. He rolled flat on his back, pulling her on top. She loved the feel of him beneath her.

She explored his chest with her hands. He was hard and muscular and very much a man, with a smattering of hair that arrowed down to his jutting sex. The brush of his hair-roughened thighs against her smooth—recently shaved, thank goodness—legs intensified her own femininity. She moved against him and felt the thrust of his arousal.

He caught one end of the ribbon holding her lingerie together and tugged. Hooking his thumbs in the satin straps on her shoulders, he slid them down her bare arms, the front unlacing along the way. She shrugged it off the rest of the way.

Olivia sighed at the play of skin against skin. With no clothes between them, they leisurely explored one another. His fingers following the curve of her back, the indent of her waist. Olivia discovered a small scar, finding the puckered flesh as she caressed the warm velvet of his back. Between kisses he murmured honeyed words that touched her soul and unleashed her passion. Words that praised. Words that encouraged. Words that excited.

The cool tangle of sheets about Olivia's feet were in direct contrast to the heat of her pirate's warm satin skin. She extricated her foot and pushed the sheets off the end of the bed. She'd lived a lifetime of cool, crisp sheets and perhaps there was a lifetime yet to come, but tonight there was no room in her bed for cool.

Adam reached beside the bed and extracted a square foil. "It's too easy to forget to stop later," he murmured as he donned the condom.

Apprehension surged through her. How could she have been so careless a few minutes ago? Adam ran his hands down the length of her back and back up again. *Ahh. That was how.* There was no changing the past and they were protected now. He wasn't a stranger and he was a regular blood donor. She gave herself over to the moment.

Olivia circled the pucker of his male nipple with her tongue and felt the quiver that rippled through his powerful body. "Are you always so prepared, or were you that sure of me?"

He buried his hand in her hair and brought her face to his. "You've always been a fantasy, but never a sure thing."

The quiet force of his words thrilled her, emboldened her. She'd never considered she might be anyone's fantasy.

Adam guided her to her side and gentled her hair to one shoulder. Using his lips and tongue, he feted the nerve-rich back of her neck. The mattress pressed against her cheek, muffling her sighs and moans whispered into the dark as gooseflesh prickled her skin. She'd never realized pleasure could be so exquisite as to border on pain.

She rolled onto her belly and clutched at wrinkled, warm cotton when he trailed his mouth down the sensitive line of her spine. His beard rasped against her soft flesh, an erotic contrast to his smooth lips.

With husky, honeyed words, he paid tribute to her. Each murmured phrase, each brush of his lips, tightened the tension inside her.

He discovered the dimples bordering her buttocks. His tongue dipped and swirled in the slight indentations, sending heat spiraling through her. He cupped the mounds of her cheeks and lavished them with sucking kisses. Instinctively, she hiked her rear closer to the source of such gratification. The tip of his tongue probed her cleft and nearly rendered her insensate.

Enough. Any more titillation and she'd explode. She whirled upright and pushed him to his back, her breath coming in ragged pants. Adam laughed, low and wicked. "You have the most delectable ass, Lady Olivia," he murmured as he encircled her wrist and drew her on top of him.

His words proved lie to her earlier thought that she couldn't grow more aroused. She could. She abandoned any latent inhibitions and all coherent thought as she took him deep within her body.

Adam filled her and still it wasn't enough. Even as her muscles gripped him, she hungered for him with an ache that transcended the physical. Their measured rhythm gave way to a frantic, almost violent battle of give and take. She rode him, each plunge bringing her pleasure, yet intensifying her craving for more.

Adam rolled her nipples between his thumbs and forefingers, bringing a sharper edge to her desperate quest.

"Liv, come with me to a place only the two of us can go," his harsh voice beseeched her. "Let me take you there."

It was as if Adam's words unlocked a place she'd carefully guarded. Olivia opened her heart and soul to the man beneath her, inside her, who this night had touched her as no one had ever touched her before. As she gave herself over to the spasms of physical release, her spirit soared, assuaging the ravening hunger that had gripped her.

Chests heaving, panting, sweating, they collapsed against one another, Adam cradling her against him. Neither spoke into the sated, emotional silence that connected them.

Tonight had been perfect. Still lying on top of him, the two of them still joined in the most intimate way, Olivia rested her head on the broad expanse of his chest. The steady rhythm of his heartbeat lulled her into further contentment. Adam's big hand rubbed lazy circles down her spine.

The bedside phone trilled into the thick, satisfied silence. Adam's hand stilled. "Do you need to get that?"

"Uh-uh. Let the machine get it. I'm not moving." Olivia sighed, stirring his chest hair to tickle her nose. Probably Marty, all liquored up, in jail and needing her to bail him out. Again. She should pick up the phone so Adam wouldn't hear the call from Inmate Marty at the Colther County Jail. But it was just too darn much trouble to move. And a drunk brother in the pokey didn't seem such a big deal when you were lying naked on top of a pirate who'd just plundered you beyond satisfaction.

Fourth ring and the answering machine took over. Even her voice, instructing the caller to leave a message, didn't sound so squeaky when she was lying naked on top of the man dedicated to her own personal pillage.

"Olivia, it's Adam." Adam? It couldn't be.

Contentment. Lethargy. Satisfaction. Sanity. All vanished with those three little words.

Adam was.... His voice came through loud and clear over the answering machine. "Once again, I'm sorry I couldn't come tonight. I left a message earlier. I hope you had a good time, anyway." She missed the rest of the message as a loud buzzing filled her brain and she fought overwhelming panic.

For one second, or perhaps a lifetime, the magnitude of her mistake paralyzed her.

Even as the penis buried deep inside her shrank to...well, the proportions of most men...Olivia flung herself off of the naked stranger and scrambled for her glasses.

Hands shaking, she shoved aside her mask, put on her

glasses, and fumbled for the lamp. Hell's bells. She was naked. Olivia grabbed one corner of the rumpled sheet and covered herself. The first thing that registered in the lamplight was the tattoo on the muscular arm that had so recently held her. *Born to Raise Hell.*

Olivia closed her eyes for one second and blinked them open again. Nope. He was still there. This was a nightmare, but she wasn't gonna wake up.

She was wearing a sheet and a naked, tattooed man was boldly stretched out on her bed. Her starched dress lay beneath her feet in a heap, crumpled beyond recognition.

With sinking heart, Olivia voiced the question, even though she knew the answer. "If that was Adam, who the hell are you? And what are you doing here?"

4

"I CAN EXPLAIN." Luke leaned back on his arms. No need to introduce himself, he'd seen recognition flash in her eyes, followed by loathing.

"How could you do this? You masqueraded as your brother and then you...we..." Her gaze swept the rumpled bed. Flushed, she clutched the sheet tighter around her.

"Yes, we did." The scent of their lovemaking surrounded them. "And it was very, very good." His voice ended on a low, rough note as he sat there, damn close to stupefied by the portrait of Olivia against the backdrop of her elegant bedroom, her hair tangled about her shoulders and her kiss-swollen lips at odds with her prim tortoiseshell glasses. Sexy as hell, that's what she was. Want unfurled low in his belly. Unfortunately, he'd have about a snowball's chance in hell of talking her back into bed right now. *Maybe ever.* He forced his attention away from the curve of her breasts outlined by the sheet and the fine bones in her hand clutching said sheet.

Awareness mingled with the anger and betrayal that simmered beneath her surface. Olivia's gaze flickered over him. Hell yeah, it had been better than good between them. Even now, all she had to do was look at him and he wanted her again. Maybe his libido was making up for lost time. Or maybe she just made him crazy. Either way, she was looking and he was starting to stand at attention. Her nipples peaked into relief against the sheet, revealing her own response.

Feeling at a distinct disadvantage lying about with a hard-on, Luke swung his legs over the side of the bed and picked up his briefs. "I'd better put these on."

Olivia's posture grew ramrod straight. "I'm perfectly capable of restraining myself."

He stood and pulled on his briefs and pants, deliberately eyeing the pout of her nipples through the fabric. "Good for you. I'm not so sure I am."

The rapid rise and fall of her chest and her unsteady hand clutching her sheet told a different story. She marched across the room and wrenched open a door. Poised on the bathroom threshold, she turned to face him once again, regal in her makeshift cotton toga and mussed hair. "I'm getting dressed. Then you're going to tell me why you did this and then you can get out." The door closed with a click, more telling than if she'd slammed it.

Luke shrugged into the shirt draped over the edge of the bed. Things had gotten out of hand and gone much further than he'd planned, but there was something to be said for the old adage of taking two to tango.

He traced a finger along the intricate carvings of the bedpost, polished to a high gloss. Mahogany. His granddaddy Joe had whittled and taught Luke all about woods. This particular wood was beautiful, with subtle patterns in its grain, yet strong and resilient.

The red light of the answering machine blinked from the nightstand. Adam. It confirmed that he, Lucas Jasper Rutledge wasn't a decent person. A decent person would've felt a hint of guilt over stealing his brother's girlfriend. And she was stolen, whether she knew it or not. Adam had crossed the line when he'd referred to

her as the "ice princess" in his disdainful tone. Olivia—
a far cry from an ice princess—deserved better than that.
Even he, Luke, was better than that.

The door across the room opened and Olivia the Librarian emerged—hair scraped back in a low, tight bun,
her body covered by a long skirt and loose shapeless
sweater. Luke was sure she'd deliberately outfitted herself to be as nondescript as possible. She could waltz out
wearing a tent and it wouldn't matter. The image of her
by the bed, brimming with tousled sensuality, was
burned into his brain. He would forever know the
woman beneath whatever clothes or mask she chose.

"The den's this way." Olivia avoided looking at the
rumpled bed. Shoulders stiff, she led him down the
short hall, past the scene of the first crime—the front
door—and into a room lined floor-to-ceiling with
shelves of books except for one shelf dedicated to an
aquarium stocked with a colorful array of fish. Two arm-
chairs flanked the fireplace. A small lamp cast a dim
glow over the back of one of the chairs and a fat, sleeping cat. Stacks of books spilled over onto the floor next to
a plump sofa which faced the chairs and fireplace. Except for Olivia's hostility, the room held a cozy intimacy,
which she immediately dispelled by turning every lamp
in the room on high. The orange-striped cat blinked in
the sudden harsh glow of several sixty-watts.

She perched on the edge of the cat chair. "Sit or
stand." He took a step toward her and she threw up a
slender arm as if to ward him off. "As long as you're not
near me."

Luke opted for the sofa.

"Now, maybe you wouldn't mind explaining why
you decided to ruin my life." Tight anger laced her voice

and glittered in her eyes. The cat stretched and hopped off the back of her chair. Smart cat.

Damn, wasn't that a bit harsh? "I wouldn't consider sleeping with me ruining your life."

"I've been dating your brother. Finding myself in bed with you is a disaster." Her hands gripped the chair arms until her knuckles turned white and her face turned red.

Even Luke's thick hide objected to being labeled a disaster. "Well, sugar, landing in the sack with you wasn't exactly where I planned to be either. Believe it or not, I didn't set out to corrupt you, Lady Olivia."

"Well." Color flushed along her cheekbones. "What exactly does that mean?"

He was damned if he did and damned if he didn't. If he burst her bubble and told her the "good brother" she'd been dating, the respectable one, was only using her, she'd never believe him. He opted for the other damnation. "It means I went to the party in Adam's costume, but I never meant for things to go as far as they did."

"You deliberately tricked me. You know I'd never come near you with a ten-foot pole."

Damn. That hurt. "Thanks for clearing that up for me in case I might've thought otherwise."

She stood and paced back and forth in front of the empty fireplace. A coffee table, littered with a half-finished jigsaw puzzle and its pieces, separated them. She'd tugged back her hair and clothed herself in that long skirt and sweater, but she'd left her feet bare. Olivia's feet were sexy, well-shaped with bright red toenails and slim ankles. She rubbed at her temples with her fingertips. "Oh, God, when I think what we...I may be sick."

Sick? Ouch. Olivia didn't bother to pull her punches. And yes, he had pretended to be Adam, but he didn't deserve this blistering. "I tried to tell you, Liv. More than once."

"Really?" She dropped her hands from her temples and pushed her glasses onto her nose. "How difficult was it to work in the truth somewhere between slipping into the party and slipping on the condom?" She planted her hands on her hips and glared a challenge across the coffee table.

He leaned forward, bracing his forearms against his knees. "A lot harder than you make it sound now. I tried to tell you in the garden and then again here."

"But you didn't." Her accusation hung between them. "Why did you do this? Why did you let it go so far?" She dropped back into her chair, like an engine running out of gas.

Dammit, didn't she have a clue? She'd been there with him. She'd felt it too. "I didn't know how much I would want you, after just one kiss. I didn't realize I would ache for you, like a physical pain."

The pulse at the base of her neck took on a frantic quality and she moistened her lips with the tip of her tongue, but still she gave no quarter. "That's not good enough."

No, he never had been, had he?

"What about you, Lady Olivia?"

Her head tilted in regal inquiry.

"Did you really think I was Adam? Did you really not know or did you just not want to know?"

"Of course I thought you were Adam. I can't see without my glasses." Her voice shook and she shoved her glasses farther onto the bridge of her nose. "Whether you meant for things to go that far or not, *you* made a decision. But you took away my decision, didn't you?"

Anger welled within him. She had responded to *him*. She had wanted *him*. She could at least admit that much. "Are you saying one man's touch affects you the same way? You couldn't tell the difference between my kiss and Adam's? Even now, I can still taste you, feel your fingers whisper against my skin, and it's like a potent, addictive drug. Sugar, I'll never mistake another woman for you—for the way you taste, the way you feel. Do you moan in the back of your throat for him? You know, the way you moaned for me when my tongue touched yours?"

She looked away from him. The thought that the answer might be yes sucker punched him.

"Does he taste the same as me? Smell like me? Do you want him so badly when he brings you home that the two of you barely make it inside?" She steadfastly refused to answer or meet his gaze, but her breathing rasped into the silence.

A relentless need to have her admit he affected her differently from Adam, drove him to push her. "Does he make you wet the way I do?"

She looked at him then, her eyes tortured. "Stop." Her whisper rang as loud as a shout.

"Then answer me, dammit."

"No." She leaped to her feet. "Are you satisfied? No, no and no." Her outburst filled the small room.

He hated the shame that shadowed her face and slumped her shoulders—hated that he'd put it there. "Don't look that way, as if you're ashamed of the way I make you feel."

"What do you possibly know about the way I feel?"

Disdain lifted her chin. "Does Adam know about this?" She gestured toward his costume.

"No. I overheard him. I knew he couldn't make the party."

"Would you at least have the decency to not tell him what happened tonight?"

"Even I can muster that much decency." A little sarcasm went a long way. "I'll tell him I followed you home to make sure you got here safely." He hated to do it, but he had to ask, "Are you still going to see him?"

"About the same time I go on one of those late-night TV talk circuses." She crossed the room. "I think you pretty effectively killed that relationship." Relief flooded him. "Get out of my house. If I ever lay eyes on you again, it'll be too soon."

Pretty perverse that even with her kicking him out, he planned on her laying more than eyes on him in the near future. He rounded the sofa and paused to let her walk through the doorway ahead of him.

"What about Grandma Pearl's birthday celebration tomorrow? Adam will wonder if you don't show up."

"He hasn't invited me." Triumph and relief threaded her words.

"Oh, yes he did. It's on the machine."

She stopped in her tracks. "Oh, no. And you're going to be there?" The thought appeared to nauseate her.

He'd never cared if the whole world considered him the bogeyman, but Olivia's disregard rankled. "She is my grandmother too."

"I suppose you're right." She headed toward the front door again, her chin thrust at a determined angle. "Well, then, after tomorrow, I never want to lay eyes on you again."

Too bad. "I start your new library wing on Monday."

"But your partner—" She whirled to face him.

"Change of plans. I'll be there."

"Switch it back to him." Was there a hint of a plea, a measure of desperation in her voice? It could only be a good thing for him that she was so eager to avoid him. At least she wasn't indifferent.

"No." He reached out and traced the curve of her cheek, warm satin over delicate bones, with the back of his right hand. She shuddered beneath his touch, her breathing shallow. "You can't ignore this thing between us."

"There's *nothing* between us."

"That's a lie and you know it. Wishing doesn't make it so." He shifted slightly until her back touched the front door. This time she was covered from head to toe, but she remembered being there an hour ago the same as he did. Despite everything that had just happened, she was turned on again. He read it in the glint in her eyes, in the subtle shift of her body against the door.

"It was so good. You were so hot and so wet and nothing's ever felt better." With each word, he moved closer until only a breath separated them. He cupped the nape of her neck in his hand, his thumb stroking the velvet smoothness. "You feel it now, don't you?" He knew she did. The wild beat of her pulse in her neck, the shallow rise and fall of her breasts, the seductive scent of her arousal, all exposed her awareness of their attraction.

With a strangled sound of fury, she buried her fingers in his hair and tugged his mouth to hers. Wrath and passion mingled with the brine of her tears as she assaulted his mouth. He cupped her bottom and pulled her tighter against him. Emotion, raw and powerful, surged between them. Olivia wrenched her mouth from his and pushed him away, her breath coming in shallow, ragged gasps. She dashed away tears with the backs of her hands, leaving black smudges beneath her eyes.

"Go." She wrenched open the door.

Luke stepped out into the cold dark that held a promise of the bitter winter to come. Olivia paused in closing the door.

"I just want to make sure you know. I hate you."

Damn good thing he wasn't overly sensitive. Actually, her words encouraged him. "There's a mighty thin line between love and hate, Lady Olivia."

"Thin, wide, invisible—it doesn't matter. I assure you, it's a line I won't cross in this lifetime!"

Crash!

Luke stared at the door she'd just slammed in his face. Unfortunately, for her, he took that as a challenge. And he loved a challenge.

OLIVIA NURSED A CUP OF TEA and stared out at her orderly backyard garden, brushed by the early light of dawn. The rest of her life was shot to hell, but at least the garden was still in good shape. Hortense wove between her legs and then nipped at her ankle, aggravated her mistress hadn't come through with wet food yet.

"Sorry, baby, Mommy's brain has taken a leave of absence." Autopilot carried her through the motions and she placed the food on the floor. Glancing up, Beth's face in the window of her back door startled her. Living two doors down from your best friend was sometimes a good thing and sometimes a bad thing. Olivia wasn't sure which one it qualified as this morning.

Beth blew in, her mouth running a mile a minute. "So, how was the big night? Was Adam wowed? Did the night end with a big bang? Was I right or was I wrong?

Did he hit you up for the nasty?'' She plopped onto one of the stools at the island. "Come on. Tell all."

Hysteria, kept at bay all throughout the night, bubbled forth. Olivia laughed until tears clogged the back of her throat, the rank of guilt and shame bitter on her tongue.

Beth danced out of her seat. "Well, come on. Don't keep me waiting. What happened that was so funny?''

Olivia had sworn last night would die with only her and Luke ever knowing the truth, but she felt as if her brain might explode if she didn't talk to someone and her best friend seemed a much wiser choice than anyone else.

"The highlight of the night was winding up in bed with Luke Rutledge. Not once, but twice." Sarcasm and semihysteria didn't mix.

Beth fell into the chair, her mouth opening and closing like a large-mouth bass before she managed actual speech. "Shit. No shit. Holy shit. You're not kidding? God, that's great." She took a closer look at Olivia's face. "No. No, that's not great? Definitely not. But was it great? What happened? Wait—" she fished in the pocket of her sweat jacket and pulled out a beat-up pack of cigarettes "—I need a cigarette."

"I thought you quit." More guilt. Not only had she betrayed Adam by sleeping with his brother and betrayed her own sense of self. Now she was driving her friend back into a nicotine frenzy.

"I did. This is an emergency." Beth herded her toward the back door. "Come on. I know I can't smoke in here."

Olivia followed her down the back steps to the patio, welcoming the cold bite of the wrought iron chair through her skirt. At least she felt marginally alive. She pulled her bare feet up onto the edge of the seat and dropped her head against her knees. God she was so tired. Everything was chaos. A lighter clicked. The acrid smoke of Beth's cigarette fouled the crisp autumn air. Olivia raised her head. "I'll take one, please."

"A cigarette?" Beth looked at her as if she'd requested a lobotomy.

"Sure." She seemed hell-bent on a path of self-destruction, she might as well go for broke.

Beth passed her lit cigarette to Olivia. "What happened?"

Olivia, who barely tolerated the odor of smoke, took a deep drag. It tasted like a dirty ashtray smelled, but a sudden rush to her head left her feeling light-headed and buzzed. And faintly nauseous. Make that definitely nauseous. She handed the burning butt back to Beth. "I don't want to throw up."

"I don't want you to throw up. I want you to talk." She flicked off the glowing tip. "It's sort of making me sick too."

Olivia focused on the birdbath ensconced in the perennial bed and absently noted she needed to deadhead the buddleia. She wanted to talk—she *needed* to talk— but she didn't think she could bear to look her friend in the face. "Adam had a sudden business meeting. Luke put on Adam's costume, drove Adam's car and came to the party. One thing led to another and we wound up here. Things got out of hand and I haven't been able to sleep all night because my bed smells like him even after I changed the sheets and I can't get away from what happened there. Then I tried sleeping on the couch, but he was sitting there so now that's contaminated. And every time I walk by the front door or see it—"

"The front door?" Beth interrupted in an awed tone. "The front frigging door? Ohmigod."

Olivia passed a weary hand over her forehead. "Yes, the front door. Get a hold of yourself. One of us has to have some wits about them, and I seemed to have lost mine."

"No, that wasn't your wits, honey," Beth quipped and then tried to look contrite. "Sorry. Never mind."

Three doors down a lawn mower roared to life. She didn't need a watch to know it was 8:45. Elridge Whitman mowed his lawn every Saturday morning at precisely 8:45. Obviously Elridge hadn't ruined his life last night, or if he had, it didn't stop him from mowing his lawn. "What am I going to do? Luke's ruined my house. I've ruined my life." She searched Beth's freckled face and brown eyes for a solution.

Beth gave a slight shake of her head. "Hold on. Before we can move on to 'what'm I gonna do?' we've got to wrap up how this happened."

"I told you."

"No, you told me one thing led to another. So, he said, 'Hiya, I'm standing in for Adam tonight, wanna head over to the stabbin' cabin and get naked?' whereupon you promptly dragged him home and proceeded to christen the front door?"

"Stabbin' cabin? Christen the front door? Remind me why we're friends, again." She pulled off her glasses and cleaned them with her sweater hem. "I thought he was Adam."

"How could you possibly mistake Luke for Adam?"

Olivia waved her glasses in the general direction of Beth's blur. "It was dark. I didn't have on my glasses." She shoved them back onto her nose and the world regained focus.

"I hate to bring this up, but what about when he kissed you? Wasn't it different?"

Which was essentially Luke's defense earlier. How could she make them understand something she could barely reconcile? Something she'd berated herself for throughout the early morning hours.

"Of course it was different. But then everything else was as well. We were both in costume. There was almost something magical about it all." No one seemed to understand. She wasn't even sure she did anymore. She should have known the difference.

"Hmmm." Beth pursed her lips. "Magical. Now that's interesting. I knew Luke would be a better kisser. And if you're this wigged out, I hope at least it was good." Beth sighed. "Twice, and one of those against the door. It must've been very good."

"That's one of the most miserable parts. What kind of woman has great—beyond great—sex with a man she absolutely loathes?" She'd finally crossed the line she'd toed for so long and lived down to everyone's expectations. "Perhaps Amy Murdoch was right all those years ago. Even after I knew who he was, I still wanted him. That's why I couldn't sleep in my bed or on that couch because he was there and it's as if he gave me an itch only he can scratch." She raised a shaking hand to her head. "The next thing you know, I'll be buying a halter top and dying my hair."

"Damn, Skippy. You've got it bad. Real bad. What's the problem with letting him scratch that itch again?"

"Shall I start at the top of the list? I don't like him."

"Who says you've got to like him? Do you want him to scratch your itch or engage in deep conversation? Men do it all the time—sleep with women they wouldn't take home to meet their mother because the sex is good."

Olivia wrinkled her nose in distaste. "I'm not into recreational sex. And even if I were, there's the little matter of me having dated his brother. It strikes me as a wee tad tacky."

"Lucky call, if you ask me—"

Her frayed nerves weren't up to Beth maligning Adam. "Don't start again about Adam."

"What are you going to do about *him?*"

Her emotions were such a jumbled mess, she couldn't seem to sort herself out. "I don't know. I care about him. I thought we had a future together. But how could I ever be intimate with him after Luke? Every time he touched me, guilt would consume me." *And would that be because Luke had touched you in the past or because you'd wish he was touching you now instead of Adam?*

"I bet he wouldn't be nearly as good in the sack as Luke," Beth came close to reading her traitorous mind.

Olivia buried the horrid thought. "There's no way I can continue to see Adam. But if I break it off suddenly, he'll be suspicious." She shuddered at the thought of Adam finding out she'd slept with Luke. "I'm supposed to go to his grandmother's birthday party today. They'll both be there. I'm a wreck. But I can't not go. His grandmother's donated quite a bit of money to the new library wing." She felt physically ill at the consequences of her mistake. "Could my life possibly take on a more tawdry aspect?"

"Sure, it could be worse. What if Adam had walked in on you instead of calling." Beth paused for a breath and peered at Olivia beneath her fringe of bangs.

Olivia buried her head in her hands.

"Okay, never mind." Beth patted her back.

Olivia looked up. "What was I thinking last night? For one evening I lost my mind and now I've made a hash of everything." She pulled her head out of her hands. "You know what Colther County is like. If this gets around, I could lose my job. Small towns aren't big on having their librarian double as the town tart. What would happen to the literacy program, the kids after-school reading program...." *Her self-respect?* She raised her chin a notch. "And I refuse to fuel the gossip fires."

"Honey, you have landed yourself in something of a mess."

"You're right. I got myself into a mess, now I've just got to dig myself out." Olivia sat up straight, placing her feet on the cold, smooth patio stones.

"That's my girl." Beth scooted to the edge of her seat. "How're you gonna do it?"

"It's simple really. I'm just going to pretend it never happened. It's gone. Wipe the slate clean. I'll gradually break things off with Adam. I'll ignore Luke and everything will be fine."

Beth leaned back, wearing a smug look. "Ah, the avoidance theory. Good luck."

She lost some of the wind in her sail. "What does that mean?"

"It means some things are too big to ignore. I think this thing with Luke may be one of them."

This thing with Luke? He'd essentially made the same reference. "There is no *thing* with Luke, except a mistake made last night." There simply couldn't be a thing with Luke. An encounter—or two if you counted that first kiss thirteen years ago—was not going to destroy her self-perception. She wouldn't allow it. She would not let this get the best of her. She would eradicate Luke from her life. She could sit around whining and moaning or she could take action. If she spotted a weed taking over in her garden, she didn't just sit around complaining about it. She yanked it out. One of those wild impulses that occasionally punctuated her calm struck suddenly. "And I know just where to start."

"You do? Where?"

She'd eliminate all traces of Luke. Ready to take action, Olivia pushed to her feet. "A little exorcism will go a long way."

Beth quirked a red eyebrow, standing slowly. "Olivia, are you sure you feel okay?"

"I'm going to be just fine." She smiled grimly over her shoulder just to prove her point.

Beth shook her head, but followed nonetheless.

Olivia marched through the kitchen into her postage-stamp laundry room. Beth stood in the door, wide-eyed, while Olivia gathered a measuring tape and her drill. She already felt notably better. Suitably armed, she headed for the front door, grabbing the cordless phone on the way.

She speed-dialed the local hardware store. "Harold? Hi, this is Olivia Cooper. Can you send over a..." she held the phone on her shoulder and checked the door width with her tape measure "...let's see, a thirty-six inch, right-hand exterior door this morning? Wood. Six-panel. Half an hour? Great. I'll be here."

She hung up the phone.

"Why do you need another door?" Beth asked.

"This one's tainted," Olivia reasoned, and then proceeded to remove the hardware and take the door off the hinges. She felt positively giddy, all because she was in control—taking action and moving forward. And maybe sleep deprivation played a minor roll in her giddy state as well.

Olivia hefted the power drill. "You do have a set of your own power tools, don't you? They're empowering—no pun intended. You never know when you'll need to replace a door."

"You've lost it," Beth opined as she helped Olivia wrestle the door through the house and into the backyard. Olivia settled the door onto the edge of the patio and went in search of the cordless phone once again. Where had she left it?

"Nope. Just getting my life back in order. Soon last night will merely be a blip on the radar screen of my life." She found the phone on the floor by the now-gaping hole that used to be the front door. "One down, two to go."

She traipsed through the house and fished the phone book out of a kitchen drawer. Flipping through, she found the number for the one and only furniture company in town.

"Mike? Olivia Cooper here. Can you deliver a mattress and sofa this morning? And can you take the old mattress and sofa and drop it off at the shelter?" Luckily she frequented Mike's store and had recently shopped a new sofa. She worked through the details and hung up.

Beth gaped in her direction and then shook her head as if to clear it. "Did you or did you not just buy a sofa?"

"I did. It's a camelback upholstered in a lovely buttery chenille—"

"That's nice. You sound like an infomercial." Beth interrupted her sofa description. "But you just dropped a wad of money on a brand-new sofa and a mattress."

"What? Can't a woman make a few interior changes? That's what I have a savings account for—emergencies. This qualifies as an emergency."

Beth shrugged. "Suit yourself. I've just never seen you like this. But then again, you've never had sex against your front door with Luke either, have you?"

Put like that it sounded wicked and a bit tawdry and a ribbon of desire curled through her.

"I already regret telling you that." She seemed to be dining on regret this morning. Olivia trekked out the back door and across the dew-damped grass to the garden shed tucked on the back of her property. She knew exactly where to find the red, plastic gasoline can.

"What are you doing? You're not going to cut the grass are you?" Beth took a step back. "You've got that look."

"No, I'm not mowing the lawn. And I've got what look?" She opened the gas can.

"That same look you had right before you decked Bennie at the senior class picnic. That same look when you signed up to jump out of that plane."

Beth hadn't approved of her skydiving. Olivia doused her former front door, now in the middle of her backyard, with gasoline, running a small trail of gas out into the grass. She turned to Beth and extended her hand, palm up. "Can I borrow that lighter?"

"Is 'no' an option?"

Olivia waggled her fingers. Beth reluctantly handed it over.

One flick, a short race down the trail and flames engulfed the door in a tremendous whoosh. Bright orange flames skittered across the surface in a macabre dance, throwing off a warming heat. The fire snapped and crackled across the painted wood.

"Wow!" Beth breathed next to her. "I can't believe you really did it."

Olivia swiped her hands together in satisfaction. She would chalk last night and Luke Rutledge up to one huge mistake and move on. Her life could return to its nice even keel.

Just as soon as she got through Adam, Luke and the party this afternoon.

5

Luke blasted down the tree-lined, quarter-mile stretch of River Oaks's driveway, savoring the last seconds of the wind stinging against his face and the roar of his bike. He eased off the gas and killed the engine, parking on the concrete slab behind Adam's car instead of inside the garage. Until last night, when Olivia had usurped the position, riding his bike had been a pleasure second to none.

He kicked the stand into place and got off, hanging his helmet over the handlebar. Early afternoon sun glinted off the low-slung chrome and black metal. His truck was a piece of crap, but his bike was a beauty. He pulled out a thin cigar and lit it. As he dropped the lighter back into his pocket, Adam rounded the garage corner.

"I can't believe you drove my car and wore my costume. No one drives my car." He buffed an imaginary spot on the Beemer's trunk. "And I was saving that costume."

Luke didn't ask how Adam knew he'd been to the party. It had never been his intent to keep it a secret. Apparently his little brother was far more concerned about his car and costume than his girlfriend. "Your car needs a tune-up and the pants were too tight." Luke narrowed his eyes and grinned around his cigar. "But I liked the sword and the eyepatch."

"How'd you know I wasn't going to the party?"

Adam might be a whiner, but he wasn't stupid. Luke shrugged as he unstrapped Grandma Pearl's present from the back of his bike.

"I didn't. But it seemed like the pirate thing to do." He'd done enough wild and crazy things earlier in his life, he knew his explanation would wash. Despite his success, he'd set his course. No one in his family, or the town for that matter, expected rational behavior from him.

"Well, you could've asked."

"But that wouldn't have been very piratelike, would it?"

Adam assumed a telling nonchalance. "Did you talk to anyone at the party last night while you were me?"

Like your contact? "A couple of people."

Adam slicked back his already slicked hair. "Really? Who?"

"Some guy dressed like a marshmallow. And Henrietta Williams tried to set you up with Candy."

"You didn't..."

Damn. He should have. "Nah. You're safe."

"Anyone else?"

"Just Olivia." He kept his voice neutral and watched Adam's face for any hint of tenderness or caring.

No such animal crossed Adam's features. "Oh, yeah. Olivia."

"So, what's up with you and Olivia? Since when have you gone slumming, bro?" Luke baited him, watching for Adam's reaction. Personally, if anyone referred to Olivia as slumming, brother or not, he'd rearrange a few body parts for them.

"We've been dating a few weeks. I believe I've been a good influence on Olivia." Adam picked a piece of lint off his starched button-down with the hoity-toity designer logo on the pocket. "Although her family's beyond hope." Adam's snobbery was palpable.

"I was surprised. She doesn't seem your type," Luke pressed.

"She's a whole lot more appealing when you realize her family's sitting on a prime piece of real estate." Adam smirked.

Bingo. "So is it the land or the lady?"

"Maybe it's a package deal."

"Since when is the Cooper place prime real estate?"

"It's all in who you know."

Luke grunted. If he showed too much interest, Adam might clam up.

"What did you and Olivia talk about last night? You know, she doesn't particularly like you."

He was already very clear on that point. "Thanks for making sure I knew. We didn't talk too much." No, they'd been far too busy with other things. "We danced one dance. She was ready to leave and I followed her home to make sure she got there okay."

"I'm not surprised she wanted to leave early. I'm sure she was disappointed when she found out it was you instead of me."

"She was definitely surprised. And she seemed to have a fever." The devil inside prompted him.

A frown creased Adam's forehead—annoyance, not concern. "I hope she can make it today." Luke silently thanked his brother for laying to rest any vestige of doubt that he'd wronged Olivia by coming between her and Adam. Adam wasn't fit for her to wipe her feet on. "Was she feeling better when you left?"

"She didn't say."

"I really wanted her to come today." The note of exasperation in his voice was reinforced by another frown.

"I'm sure she'd hate to inconvenience you by being sick." Adam seemed oblivious to the sarcasm.

"You're right. I've got some paperwork to finish before the party or I'd go check on her. Hey, could you...never mind. I won't ask you to go. You know, she doesn't like you."

Nah. That wasn't true. According to Lady Olivia herself, she hated him. He reminded himself once again of that thin line....

SHE HATED LUKE RUTLEDGE.

Olivia reluctantly crossed the wide expanse of immaculately kept lawn that stretched between the tree-lined driveway and the massive double front doors of the Rutledge home. Under normal, rational circumstances, she would be dancing across the grass...well, probably not dancing but pretty darned excited at being invited to Grande Dame Pearl Rutledge's birthday celebration. *Mais non.* Thanks to Luke, she'd prefer facing down a firing squad. Nothing quite like an incredible night with the wrong brother to throw a spanner in the works.

As she reached for the lion-head door knocker, the door swung open. "Welcome to River Oaks," the uniformed doorman intoned.

Olivia bit back a snort of laughter at the sight of her second cousin, once removed, decked out in a butler's uniform. "Hi, Ralphie."

"Hey, Olivia." Ralph smoothed a hand over his black jacket. "Pretty nice outfit, huh? You working the party too?"

After a fashion, but she didn't think that's what Ralphie meant. She hefted the gift-wrapped box. "I'm a guest."

Ralph looked as if she'd declared a UFO sighting. "Here? At River Oaks?"

"No, at Lorraine Kendall's. I just showed up here, instead. Of course here at River Oaks," she snapped, feeling more like a freak by the second. She immediately felt contrite. It wasn't Ralphie's fault she didn't belong here. It wasn't his fault that it was much more natural for her family members and herself to attend a River Oaks party as staff rather than guest. It wasn't his fault she'd had two hours of sleep. Nor was it his fault she'd spent those two hours dreaming about breaking in her new bed with Luke. "I'm sorry, Ralphie. I'm tired and grumpy." And essentially losing her mind.

"No prob. I know how your side of the family can get." To make up for being a grump, she let his comment pass. "The party's down the hall, first ballroom on the right."

First ballroom? There was more than one? Olivia stepped into the pink, marbled foyer with its soaring ceiling resplendent with plasterwork. Twin staircases with ornately carved mahogany banisters polished to a mirror finish curved gracefully to the second floor. How many times, as a little boy, had Luke slid down that banister? This is where Luke...and Adam...had grown up.

"Watch out. The punch in the silver bowl is spiked. You definitely want the one in the clear glass bowl." Ralphie's whisper echoed in the cavernous room.

Light reflecting off the massive chandelier's hundreds of prisms dazzled and distracted her. Not even a hint of duct tape holding anything together here. She could definitely relate to the fish out of water. "Uh, thanks, Ralphie."

Five minutes. She just had to make it through the next five minutes, ten minutes tops. She'd drop off the gift, wish Mrs. Rutledge many happy returns, make some excuse to Adam and be on her way.

Ralphie nudged her toward the hall beneath the twin staircases. A group crowded a doorway from which spilled all the sounds of a tasteful party in progress—laughter, muted music, the odd clink of glasses. "Last I heard, no one in there bites." His reassuring smile revealed a missing eyetooth.

"Let's hope you're right." Still she stood rooted to the spot, feeling gauche and decidedly out of place.

"I believe you've asked everybody in there at one time or another for money for that library of yours. They ain't no different now than they were then."

"I believe you're right." She was being utterly ridiculous. She'd already spent two minutes standing around dithering when she could have been fulfilling her social obligation, bringing her two minutes closer to leaving. Olivia squared her shoulders, called in every measure of courage she possessed, and marched down the hall.

Ballroom number one. Open double doors. A five-piece ensemble playing dinner music. A parquet dance floor. A table running the length of one wall laden with what was probably a mouthwatering assortment of food if one wasn't nauseous with nerves. About one hundred and fifty or so of Dame Rutledge's closest friends and family standing about in clustered groups. It looked as if she'd found the right place.

She slipped into the room. Maybe she'd get lucky and not even see Luke.

But then again, maybe not. Because there he was, looking every inch the reprobate. Her stomach flip-flopped at the sight of him. Long legs encased in worn jeans, black T-shirt hugging his muscular back, his hair carelessly pulled back, similar to his pirate's style last night. A gold earring glinted in one ear. He looked lean, hard and dangerous.

Impossible. Ridiculous. He stood across the room milling with groups of people, but she swore she could smell his masculine scent. Her response was unnervingly Pavlovian as a shiver chased down her spine, stirring an ache deep inside. At that instant, he turned and looked directly at her, as if she'd beckoned him.

"How about a glass of punch, little lady?" a friendly voice offered.

From across the room, Luke's eyes swept her from head to toe and back again, a crooked smile lifting one corner of his mouth. Her body reacted as if he'd flipped a switch and turned her on. His look warmed her from the inside out.

She swallowed hard, her mouth dry, her pulse racing. She turned to find a vaguely familiar man beside her, just a few inches taller than herself, sporting a waxed handlebar mustache. "Jack Rutledge, at your service." He offered a stiff bow from the waist. "But I'd be honored if you'd call me Uncle Jack."

"Olivia Cooper. Pleased to meet you. And, yes, a glass of punch would be great." Luke glanced from her to the door and back again, a wicked grin on his face. The clear bowl had the rum kick, didn't it? Good lord, how could she think clearly with him conjuring up memories of the door and the two of them.... "From the silver bowl, if you don't mind."

Two seconds before she'd felt relatively in control. She'd deliberately selected an outfit that didn't call attention to herself. A long navy skirt—no slits up the sides—navy flats, a gray twinset and pearls. But with just one look and a lazy smile from Luke, she felt downright sexy. With the slightest shift the silk and angora blend of her sweater caressed her skin, teasing against suddenly sensitive flesh. What had a minute ago been a sensible navy skirt, now slid sensuously against her thighs and teased against her buttocks.

She fought the urge to flee. Last night had been an anomaly, an aberration. A mixture of magic brought on by the costume and the moon. How in the world could she feel sexy covered head to toe in waning daylight in the middle of an octogenarian birthday party?

"Here you are, miss." Uncle Jack held out a medium-sized glass filled with pink punch.

She took the proffered drink and sucked down half the punch at once. Cool and refreshing, it tingled against her tongue as if it contained an extra bottle of effervescent ginger ale. Yum-o. She killed the rest of the cup. "Thank you. I was thirstier than I realized. That's refreshing."

"They've got bigger glasses, if you're still thirsty." Uncle Jack appeared eager to fetch more.

It was so nice to find someone who was...well, so nice. Unlike Luke, who was so annoying, duplicitous, unsettling, arousing.... "Only if you're having one as well."

Uncle Jack hoisted his glass and drained it in a single swallow. "I'll be back in a jiffy."

Olivia smiled her appreciation and found a wall to hold up. Often it was nice to fade into the background—never a difficult task for her—and watch the world around her.

She scanned the room, eager to look somewhere other than at Luke's darkly handsome face and eyes full of memories and intent. A tight cluster of women stood a few feet away. Her high school nemesis, Amy Murdoch-Carter, held court with her cronies. Olivia noted, with no small measure of satisfaction, that Amy's behind had grown considerably wider since their high school days. In fact, her butt tested the stretchability of her black knit skirt. Olivia might be white trash in Amy's book, but at least Olivia had enough decorum not to appear with her ass threatening to break free of the bonds of interlock confinement.

"Here we are, my girl. Hell of, er heck of, a line over there." Uncle Jack offered her another cup. He had the nicest, brightest eyes.

"Thank you, kind sir." Something dangerously close to a giggle escaped her, but Olivia shrugged it off. Uncle Jack put her at ease.

She glanced toward Luke. He began walking in her direction. Finally, Olivia noticed the man beside him. Adam. Olivia swallowed a double measure of guilt and washed it down with punch. She should've naturally noticed Adam before she noticed Luke. Her eyes should have sought him from the moment she arrived.

Now, not only were they both at the same party, they were both heading straight for her. Feeling detached and curiously calm, she watched dear, sweet, starched and tailored Adam with his pungent hair gel stroll beside his immoral, tattooed, rogue, sexy...nix sexy, hellion of a brother.

She drained her cup. Jack plucked it from her fingers. "I'll be right back."

"I'll be here." She'd definitely wait around for another glass of that. She'd ask Aunt Ruth for the punch recipe because she felt all nice and warm and actually very capable of handling this imminent encounter, albeit slightly unsteady on her feet. Amy Murdoch-Carter glanced over her shoulder at Olivia, a faux smile on her face. Olivia smiled back. Maybe she should wander over and inquire if Amy was involved in a case study testing the bounds of stretchability. Yep, that struck her as just the thing to do.

Of all the rotten timing! Just as she pushed away from the wall, Adam and Luke arrived.

"Olivia. I was beginning to get worried." Adam slid an arm around her shoulder, his lips cool as they brushed against her cheek. Beside him, Luke's mouth tightened and his eyes hardened. Olivia managed to shift out of Adam's embrace, repulsed by his touch, the cloying combination of hair gel and cologne, and her own wretched guilt. Adam reached for her hand, his soft banker's fingers smoothing against the back of her hand. "I was afraid you might still be sick. Luke said you had a fever last night."

Against her better judgment, she glanced at Luke. Devilment and a hint of anger lit the depths of his blue eyes. "Do you remember how hot you were? You were burning up."

Intense memory. Instant response. Her traitorous body quickened. Yes, she remembered. Everything. His scent. The satisfying feel of him buried deep within her. The taste of him against her tongue. If she wasn't unarmed and it wouldn't cause such a fuss, she'd kill Luke Rutledge.

"I'm fine now," she assured Adam, shooting daggers Luke's way.

"I don't know, Olivia, you look rather flushed to me and your eyes are all glittery." Adam turned to Luke. "Is this how she looked last night, when you took her home?"

Annoyance flashed through her. Adam didn't need to talk about her as if she wasn't there or was some inept child. "I said, I'm fine," she enunciated clearly, her speech a bit more difficult than usual. Maybe she was coming down with something.

Luke pressed his hard, callused fingers against her forehead. Even that minimal contact set her pulse racing. And her head spinning. Or was that the room spinning?

"I definitely think your fever is coming back. You're all flushed. And maybe a bit of difficulty breathing." He trailed his fingers across her temple and smoothed the backs of his fingers against her cheek. "You feel hot to me."

Longing rippled through her, even as heat washed over her. And horrible man that Luke was, he knew it.

Adam stepped back as if she was a leper. "You might be contagious."

"Absolutely not."

"Probably," Luke offered simultaneously.

"Maybe I should keep my distance, since I'm speaking at the Rotarian luncheon on Monday." Adam took yet another step away and pushed Luke closer. "You, however, have already been exposed, so would you mind looking after her?"

"I'm overwhelmed by your concern and compassion," Olivia quipped, her irony totally lost on Adam. "But I don't need anyone to take care of me."

"I think you're hotter than you realize." Luke's voice slid over her like satin sheets on a cool night, smooth and arousing. "And I'm a regular Florence Nightingale."

"It's not like you to be difficult, Olivia." A faint frown marred Adam's brow.

She bit back a laugh. Difficult? He thought she was being difficult? *It's also not like me to sleep with Luke.* She gritted her teeth over his patronizing air. She wouldn't have been surprised if Adam had patted her on the head and commanded her to stay, like a good dog. She opened her mouth to say so. Adam stepped back. "I see Charlie Moncrief across the room and I really need to talk to him. Luke'll take care of you and I'll call you later."

Adam slipped away before she could bark her obedience. Luckily, Uncle Jack showed up with two large glasses of punch. "Here you go. One more glass for medicinal purposes." He looked at Luke in surprise. "I see you found a girl with class for a change."

"I'm not his girlfriend," Olivia muttered before drinking some of the delicious brew, much less upset by being mistaken for Luke's girlfriend than she normally might've been. In fact, she smirked into her punch glass that she had more class than his other women. Although the idea of other women vexed her.

"Uncle Jack, *you've* been plying Olivia with punch?" A frown bisected Luke's forehead.

Olivia turned to Luke. "You know Uncle Jack?"

"He's my father's brother."

Ah, that's why Uncle Jack looked familiar. Those brilliant blue eyes belonged in the family.

Luke turned to Uncle Jack. "Is this your *special* punch?"

Olivia drank the last drop and peered from Luke to "Uncle Jack" and back again.

Uncle Jack looked a bit sheepish. "She said she wanted a drink from the silver bowl. Oops. Your grandma's waving me over with her cane. Gotta run." Uncle Jack disappeared faster than a dollar at a dog track.

She felt positively giddy. And more than a little unsteady on her feet. She clutched Luke's forearm, the hair-roughened, hard sinews beneath her fingertips sending a dizzying spiral of heat through her. "Mmm. You have very sexy arms."

"Olivia, can you do something for me?"

Any number of truly wicked thoughts came to mind. "Uh, hmm." She pushed her glasses up.

Luke led her to a chair and seated her. "Wait here for me. Don't try to get up. I'll be right back." He started to leave, but hurried back. He leaned in close, his breath stirring the hair above her ear, her senses lapping up his maleness. "Don't talk to anyone. Not a word. No one." And then he was gone.

She pursed her lips in a pout. Sitting in a chair wasn't what she'd had in mind, but she'd promised. She watched Luke make his way across the room, mesmerized by the play of cotton snugged over his broad shoulders and black denim over his tight— She lost sight of him behind a group gathered in front of the food table. She wasn't hungry at all, but she sure wouldn't mind some more punch.

Amy materialized like a bad blast from the past. "Olivia Cooper? It is you. I wasn't sure. Marvin and I made a special trip for the party. You know, we're living in Atlanta now. I didn't expect to see you here. How are you? Staying out of trouble?" She winked conspiratorially.

I'm fine. My ass isn't the size of Rhode Island these days. Luke had said she shouldn't talk. Maybe he was on to something. Olivia pointed to her throat.

"Is there a problem with your throat? You can't talk?" Amy quizzed her.

Luke reappeared over her shoulder. "Flu. Might be a bad strain."

Amy jumped back like a scalded cat. "Bye then." And

headed for the food table, towing her own small state behind her.

Luke pulled Olivia to her feet. She surged forward unsteadily. Reaching out, she braced herself against the hard wall of Luke's chest. The strong, solid beat of his heart thudded against her palm. "Easy, Lady Olivia. Let's go out this door right over here."

Olivia started to protest, but she hadn't wanted to stay for long in the first place. Leaving with Luke hadn't been part of her plan. However, it suddenly seemed like a good idea. Actually, Luke was hustling her out of the party so fast, her head was spinning. Literally.

His hand warm and firm on her arm, he led her down a back passage. Somewhere between the ballroom and the hallway, he'd morphed from dark and dangerous to solid strength. She had the oddest sense of being taken care of.

She stumbled to a halt. "Are you taking care of me?" She sounded as puzzled as she felt. "You can't, you know. That's my job. Pops. The family. The library. The literacy program. I'm the caretaker."

He resumed walking, tugging her along after him. "I don't take care of anyone. Just call this a friendly hand."

"But we're not friends. I don't like you." Just because her body went into meltdown mode when he was around didn't mean she liked him.

"That's old news. Right now, sugar, you need help from whatever quarter you can get it. Even if you consider me the enemy."

They stepped out onto a terrace overlooking a rolling meadow and the river beyond. Olivia blinked in the weak, yet sudden, sunlight.

"Why do I need help?" Outside of working very hard to pronounce all of her words.

"Because you, Lady Olivia, are snockered. Tanked. Buzzed. Plastered. Plowed. Take your pick."

"Nah." She waved a dismissing hand in the air. "Never touch the stuff." She leaned closer to his ear, her cheek brushing against the hard line of his jaw. "My family's too fond of the stuff and it makes us crazy. A wine cooler's never even passed these lips."

She presented her lips for his inspection. Luke brushed the pad of his thumb against her mouth. Longing welled inside her to the point of aching.

"These lovely lips never had some of Uncle Jack's rum punch before either. Sugar, I figure you've had the equivalent of about four stiff drinks." He nudged her in the direction of the distant garage. "And now it's time to get you home. I'll drive you and find a way back. Do you have your keys?"

They rounded the corner and Luke swore under his breath. "Your car's blocked in." He hesitated for a few seconds. "Think you can stay on the back of my bike?"

Driving herself was out of the question. She must be drunk. She felt far too light-headed and carefree to be sober. She was never either light-headed or carefree. And especially never both light-headed and carefree.

He wanted her on that huge black and chrome beast? She didn't doubt for a minute that Luke would be in absolute control of the monster, and if she held on to him, she'd be fine. A foreign sense of excitement shot through her.

"All I have to do is sit there?"

Luke nodded. "You just have to hold on to me and lean with the turns. Do you think you can do that?"

Did a chicken have lips? Well, actually she didn't think it did, but she felt absolutely capable of wrapping her arms around his firm middle and pressing her open thighs against the tight muscles of his fine butt. 'Cause a girl in need had to do what a girl in need had to do. And she had some serious needs at the moment and she'd think about them just as soon as her head cleared. "Uh-huh."

He picked up a black leather jacket from the seat and held it up. "This'll keep you from getting cold."

Olivia shrugged into it, absorbing the sensation of the supple leather against her neck. The thing swallowed her. She inhaled the heady mixture of Luke's scent mingled with the leather and drew it deep into her body, filling herself with his smell. She knew now why women liked to wear their lover's clothes. It was the next best thing to having them inside you. "But what about you? Won't you get cold?"

Luke's eyes darkened. She recognized that look. Even though she hadn't been able to see last night, she'd felt the same response.

"No. There's no danger of me getting cold. Here. Put on the helmet."

Olivia put on the helmet.

Luke eyed the long length of her straight, navy skirt. "Damn. That skirt's going to be a problem."

She'd spent a lifetime toeing some invisible line. Now she hovered on the brink of fulfilling some bad-girl-on-a-bike fantasy she hadn't even realized she owned. Nothing was going to stop her. Olivia bent down, grasping the left seams in each of her hands. She rent the material to midthigh. She did the same on the right side. She straightened. "No problem here."

Olivia smiled her satisfaction. Mr. Luke "Bad Boy" Rutledge looked a little shocked and a whole lot turned on.

"Climb on, sugar, and I'll take you for a ride."

6

"AROUND THE WAIST. Hold on around the waist," Luke shouted over the motorcycle's roar. Most of the chicks who rode bikes went in for the black leather halter tops and tight jeans and it usually looked good. But when Olivia, wearing pearls and his jacket, had ripped her skirt to reveal those luscious legs so recently wrapped around him, he'd damn near lost it. And now her hands kept drifting south. Between her fleeting touches against his crotch and the throb of the engine, he was rock-hard. He reminded himself she needed a glass of water, a couple of aspirin and a bed—alone.

He was a far cry from Dudley Do-Right, but even *he* couldn't leave her to stumble around his grandmother's party drunk. Hell, knowing her, she'd have blamed him afterwards. Adam thought she had a fever and didn't want to come near her in case he caught something. Which had left him.

Several curtains twitched in front windows as he cruised down Olivia's street. He laughed. For a good girl, she was getting into all kinds of trouble. He downshifted and pulled into Olivia's driveway for the second time in less than twenty-four hours.

He killed the engine, stilling the throb of sixty horsepower. Unfortunately, it wasn't quite so easy to turn himself off. Olivia didn't move, her arms wrapped around his waist, her open thighs cradling him from behind, her cheek pressing against his back, separated only by the thin cotton of his T-shirt. He pulled off his helmet and spoke over his shoulder.

"Olivia? You can get off now."

"I am." Her breath was warm against the chilled skin of his neck. Instead of following his directive, she nuzzled behind his ear, her breath warm and moist against his neck. "That was so much fun. We should do it again, sometime. All that power and the way the motor throbs beneath you..."

She'd felt it too. The sexual energy flowing between them, intensified by the ride on the bike. Her fingers strummed against his belly, her knuckles teasing against the thick ridge of his erection. Want swamped him. Luke closed his eyes, bit back a curse, and dredged up his last remaining measure of self-control and decency.

What he wanted to do was stay right where he was and enjoy the feel of her behind him, around him, while she murmured low in his ear and stroked him until he came. He craved her touch so badly, it wouldn't take long. But putting on a show for her neighbors wouldn't exactly endear him to her.

Instead, he moved her hands from his belly and swung awkwardly off the front of the bike, hindered by his hard-on and her on the back. "Glad you liked the ride." He wrapped his hands around her waist and plucked her from the bike, standing her in the driveway. "But now it's time to go inside."

While he spoke he unfastened and removed her helmet, loosening several fine, dark strands of hair in the process, entrapping his fingers in a web of silk. She rubbed her cheek against his hand. Twilight wrapped around them, intensifying the want between them. Behind her glasses, Olivia's eyes smoldered. She teased her tongue against the full line of her lips, wetting them with the tip.

Luke could barely breathe. His Liv had a mouth made for loving. He ached to explore the fullness of her lips and plumb the moistness of her mouth with his tongue until her lips were swollen and slick from his kisses. The wildness inside him stirred to a fever pitch. This abandon had always belonged to him, been a part of him alone. Never had another human being served as a catalyst the way Olivia did. There was a dark intimacy in sharing ownership with this woman.

"Do you want to come inside?" Her voice, husky and low, vibrated through him, stroking him.

"Yes." In the worst way.

"I don't have the new keys, we'll have to go in through the back." She tilted her head toward the front door. "Had to get a new door. You contaminated the old one."

Contaminated? She could buy a hundred new doors and it wouldn't change the course of passion flowing between them.

She slipped her hand into his, her fingers curling around his palm and led him to a gate in the high fence that screened her backyard from the street. Luke closed the gate behind them. Somewhere outside the fence, a dog barked and a car backfired. It all seemed remote. A flagstone patio ran three-quarters of the length of the back of the house. Neat flower beds bordered an immaculate, lush green lawn. Lush and green and immaculate except for the large, irregular charred spot in the middle, approximately the size of a door.

Olivia gave an exaggerated nod. "Burned the sucker. And my pima cotton sheets."

A grin spread over his face. One minute she had him

so notched up he could barely breathe and the next minute she made him laugh. Luke would bet his bike she'd never used the word "sucker" before in her life. A little rum punch and Olivia let her hair down with a vengeance.

"What?" She questioned his amusement.

"Hope you didn't burn the mattress too."

"Nah. Gave the mattress and the sofa to Goodwill. That'da been a real waste."

She'd gone to great lengths to erase his presence. Which led him to believe that this particular lady did protest too much.

She opened the back door and they stepped into a small kitchen where bold black-and-red tile flooring complemented red walls. Luke settled her onto one of two stools fronting an island, the ripped seams of her skirt providing a distracting view of smooth, shapely leg.

He made the mistake of glancing into her smokey gray eyes. Her want and need mirrored his own. She didn't have to invite him to this party twice. He stepped into the V of her legs.

Olivia twisted the front of his T-shirt in her hand and pulled him closer yet, her eyes smoldering with a sultry heat. "It's just not fair," she complained with a pretty pout as his jacket slipped off her shoulder.

He slid his hands around to unclasp her barrette, freeing the rest of her hair. He buried his hands in the silky strands, molding his fingers against her scalp. "What's not fair, Lady Olivia?"

"How can I ache for you to kiss me—" her tongue traced against his lips "—touch me—" she cupped him through his jeans "—when I just burned my door this morning because of you?"

He didn't have an answer and he wasn't too damn sure of the question because all he could think of was the heat of her hand against him, the scent of her surrounding him. The only thing he knew for sure was she seemed to want him as much as he wanted her. And he was more than happy to oblige.

Luke claimed her mouth. Her mouth opened eagerly, her tongue parrying his thrusts. She tasted of cherries and spiced rum, a potent combination.

She moaned deep in her throat and hooked one foot behind his leg to pull him nearer, even as she tugged his shirt free from his waistband. Luke crushed her to him, the hard points of her nipples branding his chest despite the layers of clothes between them. He ran one hand along the rip in her skirt, drowning in the sweet sensation of her mouth, the hot velvet skin of her thigh, the pressure of her palm against him. His fingers brushed the satin of her panties and she arched against him, the damp material telling him all he needed to know. She was ready.

He pulled his mouth away, his chest heaving with the desperate urge to breathe. Her eyes glittered with the fire he'd stoked deep within. Her lips, swollen from their kiss, glistened, moist and ready for more. He wanted her so badly, he not only strained his fly but the limits of his self-control. The butcher block counter beside them offered a quick and ready spot. In mere seconds, he could be buried deep inside the hot, slick folds of her body.

She saw his glance cut to the counter and read his intent. Her breath came in a sharp rasp of approval. "Yes."

He reached for her and something inside him snapped. "No." He shook his head and forced himself to take one step away. Luke wasn't sure which one of them was more surprised by his decision.

"It's the glasses isn't it?" Her lower lip trembled with his rejection.

Hell, he'd feel better if it was the glasses.

He already wanted her to the point he felt as if he might explode. Damnation, now she was going to cry because she thought he didn't want her.

With a muttered oath, he took her hand and placed it against the ridge straining the confines of his jeans. It wasn't subtle. In fact the gesture bordered on crude, but he was beyond subtleties and niceties and desperate to make a point and keep his sanity. "It's not the glasses."

Her hand kneaded him through the worn denim. "It doesn't feel as if there's a problem at all."

For one glorious instant, he surged against her hand and then he summoned every ounce of restraint and a few he didn't know he possessed and stepped out of her grasp.

Still sitting on the stool, she draped herself over the edge of the counter, propped on one arm, visibly confounded.

"Baby, there's almost nothing I'd like to do more than put you up on that counter and make love to you."

Her lips parted and her breath came in short pants. He'd better finish this train of thought before her obvious turn-on derailed him and blew his misguided good intentions to hell.

"But, I'm not going to. Today. One day, I want you right there." His voice was as strained as his control. "Wearing nothing but those pearls."

He had to turn his back on her or he wouldn't manage to get past the picture. He opened a cabinet but found only spices. "Aspirin?"

She pointed to the right. "Next to the sink."

He closed the door and followed her directions. He found the bottle and shook out two before he continued. "But when that day comes—" and it was only a matter of *when*, not *if* "—it won't be because rum punch has killed your inhibitions."

He ran some water into a glass and placed the glass and aspirin on the counter before her. "Take this."

Mutely she complied.

"The next time there won't be any mask, no mistaken identity, no alcohol to hide behind."

"I'm not hiding behind alcohol. You make it sound as if I meant to drink too much."

"No. It was a mistake. But I'm not going to hand you one more reason to hate me. And tomorrow morning you would."

He tugged her to her feet, his resolve tested as she swayed against him, the soft mound of her belly rubbing against his hard-on. He turned her in the direction of the hallway and her bedroom.

"Let's get you to bed."

She laughed, a soft seductive murmur. "I knew you'd see things my way."

"Alone. You're going to bed alone."

"But I do that all the time." He was damn near ecstatic to have that confirmed. He could barely stand the thought of another man touching her.

She leaned against his arm, the pebble-hard tips of her breasts scorching him. "And I'm frustrated."

"Join the club." He couldn't muster much sympathy considering his own sorry state.

"Then let's do something about it."

The curve of her behind teased against his hip. The scent of her arousal nearly obliterated rational thought.

To hell with it. She was right. She wanted him. He wanted her. Tomorrow was another day.

Luke threw open her bedroom door. The smell of plastic wrapping and new mattress assaulted him like a splash of cold water.

"You can't keep buying new mattresses." He pushed her down on the edge of the bed. She flopped backwards.

Kneeling at her feet, he grasped her slender ankle in one hand and pulled off her shoe. A high instep and that sexy-as-hell red polish on her nails tempted him. He traced a delicate blue vein with his thumb, his other hand flexing around the smooth muscle of her calf.

"Hmm," she murmured in appreciation, as her toes curled around his palm. Luke put her foot on the ground and wiped a bead of sweat off his forehead before removing her other shoe. When had it gotten so damned hot in her room? She flexed her foot against his palm and sighed in satisfaction. "Uhh, feels sooo good."

She seemed to have very sensitive feet. He'd read somewhere that the feet were an erogenous zone. At least it seemed to be the case for Olivia.

He rose from his knees and leaned over her, sucking in a fortifying breath of resolve. He'd make her comfortable and leave. Her glasses had slipped to the end of her nose and her lashes fanned over her cheeks. He balanced one knee on the mattress and reached up to remove her glasses. Her eyes fluttered open and she captured one of his hands in hers. Even sleepy, a wicked gleam shone in the gray depths as she took his thumb into her mouth and suckled it against the tender moistness of the inside of her lips.

Luke swallowed hard as he tugged his hand free and placed her glasses on the nightstand. "Behave, Lady

Olivia.'' The rush of blood below his waist threatened to prevail.

Her eyelids closed again, a slight smile curved her full lower lip, as if she quite enjoyed her newfound role of seductress. *Save it for when you're sober, baby,* he silently encouraged her.

Reaching beneath her hips, he found the zipper to her skirt and tugged it down. Olivia arched upward. Luke wasn't sure whether it was instinctive cooperation or instinctive seduction. He slid the material down past the flat slope of her middle with the indent of her navel, her bare skin unbelievably arousing against the drag of his knuckles. Past the lace edging her satin panties. His breath lodged in his throat as he tugged her skirt over her satin-covered mound. Eyes still closed, her hips undulated in mute entreaty.

The material between her thighs was darker than the rest, damp proof of her desire. Her musky female scent assaulted him. His fingers shook with the need to push aside the silky fabric and cull her honeyed desire. He could so easily bring her a release both of them would savor.

Until she was sober.

He dragged the skirt the rest of the way off and dropped it in a heap on the floor. She'd just have to sleep with her sweater and pearls on. He'd never make it through taking those off. Her dusky nipples pouting at him through lacy cups, demanding attention.... Desperate to get the hell out of Dodge, he pulled one edge of the comforter over her and almost tripped over her fat cat in his haste to get out the door.

Being noble sucked.

OLIVIA TENTATIVELY TOUCHED the floor with a toe and groped at the bedside table for her glasses. 10:08. Light filtered through the curtains. Must be morning. It wasn't dark enough to be night. She'd slept for fifteen hours, or something close to that since she wasn't exactly sure of the time when she'd passed out.

Moving with great care, she sat up, waiting for a pounding head, a churning stomach. She waited. And waited. And waited. She stood up, anticipating the onslaught of a hangover.

Nothing. Except for a dry mouth that tasted like a dirty sock had been stuffed in it, she felt fine. Olivia considered crying, but tears wouldn't change the brutal truth. All these years she'd thought she was different from her family. The clothes. Her house. The 400-thread count Egyptian cotton sheets. Her job. Her volunteer work. She'd spent a lifetime trying to prove she wasn't the little white-trash girl from the shack on the outskirts of town. But when all was said and done, they were merely tenuous props she hid behind.

She sank back onto the mattress, her face burning with the memory of Luke bringing her home. Unfortunately, she remembered every miserable detail. She'd practically begged him to make love to her. Okay, she *had* begged. Enticed. Tried desperately to seduce. She grudgingly admitted few men would've turned down such a forward invitation.

It unnerved her that Luke knew her so well. He was right. She didn't want to respect him for walking away, because then that left only herself to vilify for her behavior.

She would stay away from punch forever. The next party she went to, she'd stick with water.

The next time there won't be any mask, no mistaken identity, no alcohol to hide behind. Luke's words filled her head. As if *next time* was a given. She also clearly recalled the strained promise in his voice when he told her he wanted her on the counter. Wearing only her pearls. Heaven help her, but even now, in the face of the previous evening's humiliation, the idea aroused her. Her body, still keyed up from last night, quickened, tightening and throbbing at the thought of Luke, hot and hard, filling her while she braced against the cool, smooth tiles on top of the island. Moisture seeped onto her thighs even as she tried to dispel the image.

There wouldn't be a next time. She had no clue as to who he was the first night and yesterday she'd been inebriated. Luke was right, next time there wouldn't be a mask or mistaken identity or a rum punch haze simply because there wouldn't be a next time. There wouldn't be any making love to him in the kitchen, wearing pearls.

No, Luke threatened every aspect of the life she'd so carefully cultivated for herself. This wild ache he fostered deep inside had no business in her life. She'd never meant to start anything with Luke, but she sure as heck intended to end it.

She dragged off her sweater and underwear, her skin sensitive to the lightest brush of her hands as she took off her bra and panties. In sheer defiance, she left on her pearls. He wanted her naked, wearing only her necklace. She wouldn't run like a coward. She'd take his fantasy and make it her own.

Olivia bent to scoop her skirt up off the floor. The movement was fraught with her own brimming sexuality and need for release—the weight of her breasts as they fell forward, the swing of the rope of pearls around her neck, the upward thrust of her bare bottom.

Olivia tossed the clothes into the hamper in her closet

and crossed to the bathroom. Her breasts felt heavy and full, her thighs tingled and ached with each step.

She reached into the shower and turned on the water, allowing the temperature to adjust. Turning, her reflection in the mirror arrested her. The woman who stared back was a stranger. Full. Brimming. Engorged nipples. Rounded breasts. Smooth thighs. Aching.

She watched the woman in the mirror until the steam from the shower blurred the reflection. Stepping beneath the spray of hot water, she reveled in the sluice against her scalp and down her back, against the sensitive curve of her buttocks, the backs of her legs. She luxuriated in the sensation of water coursing over her breasts as she lathered her hair and massaged her scalp. Her vaginal muscles clenched in anticipation as she finished rinsing her hair and turned her shower massage to pulse.

Luke may have started this ache, but she could take care of it on her own. There wasn't much a pulsating shower massage couldn't handle. She leaned against the wall of the shower and embraced the relief promised by the surging stream. Cupping the weight of her breasts in her hands, she rubbed the rounded pearls against her distended nipples.

The erotic impact bowed her against the pulsing water. Olivia closed her eyes and reveled in the sensation. In her mind, Luke appeared, watching her through the steam as she toyed the pearls around and against her breasts. Without her consent, he wrestled the fantasy back from her and made it theirs. The sexual fervor inside her pitched to a higher point as she performed her solo for him.

Within seconds she shuddered her release. And it was Luke's name that echoed off the shower walls as her muscles spasmed and clenched.

7

OLIVIA TURNED OFF the water and reached for a towel and her glasses. Through the closed bathroom door, she heard the resonance of the doorbell. She wrapped her dripping hair turban style in a towel and tugged on her robe.

She opened the bathroom door and hurried down the hall. Someone pounded on the door. "Hold on. I'm coming," she yelled, belting her robe closed.

"Olivia?"

She cracked the door and peered around the edge in a combined gesture of modesty and vanity—swathed head to toe in terrycloth wasn't exactly flattering even if it was Luke and she hated him...well, not exactly hated, maybe resented was more accurate. Olivia tightened her grip on the doorknob. With a day's growth of beard, his dark hair pulled back into a ponytail and a stud glistening in one ear, he had big, bad wolf written all over him. Olivia had no intention of becoming a pork sandwich.

"What..." she squeaked. She cleared her throat and tried again. "What do you want?"

"Aren't you going to let me in?"

Letting him in took on a whole new meaning as her recently sated body responded to him. Hadn't she just vowed he was out of her life? "No. I just got out of the shower." Water puddled around her feet. "I still need to dry off."

"Honey, I don't mind at all if you're wet." His dark eyes glittered and his voice dripped seductive innuendo.

Her body quickened and tightened. Just the thought... "I'm not dressed."

"And the downside is?" Wicked intent crossed his face and lit his blue eyes. He propped one arm against the doorjamb and leaned closer. "Wet and undressed. I won't complain."

"I don't trust you." She didn't trust herself.

"Your sharp tongue wounds me, Lady Olivia. Particularly after my gallant behavior yesterday."

Did he mean because he hadn't left her to make a drunken spectacle of herself at his grandmother's party or because he hadn't taken advantage of her when she had been so clearly willing or both? She couldn't bring herself to ask.

"Thank you." Embarrassment stiffened her voice.

"The pleasure was all mine. Now can I come in?"

She cracked the door wider but clutched at her robe. "I don't think that's a good idea. I've thanked you for yesterday, so you can leave now." She, usually a role model for decorum and good manners, realized she'd just been outright rude. But she was talking self-preservation here.

"I didn't stop by for a thank-you."

As if he'd stopped by for much more than a mere show of gratitude. How could the simplest statement out of his mouth leave her quivering? Her pearls shifted against her bare skin beneath her robe.

Luke reached into the V of her robe and fingered the strand. The back of his hand and the sprinkling of stiff dark hair brushed against her skin, feather-light. Despite her recent release, his touch evoked an immediate response.

"Did you know the more you wear pearls next to your skin, the more luminous they become?"

His touch, his scent, his voice left her poised on the edge of discarding reason. Her nipples stiffened, aching for his hand to slip lower. Her thighs trembled with the memory of his touch.

"Yes. There's a chemical reaction between your body and the pearls," she rasped. She should close either the door or this conversation. Her body overrode her mind's warning.

All playfulness disappeared. "Chemical reactions can be intense." He rolled the lustrous jewels between his fingertips, sliding the pearls against the slope of her breast exposed at the V of her robe, releasing clinging drops of water. Luke caught a drop on the tip of his finger, his touch thrumming through her body, delivering a low-voltage current of desire. "Do you always wear your pearls in the shower?"

"No." Her tongue felt thick. Swollen. He knew. He knew what she'd done in the shower as surely as if he had watched her. The knowledge glittered in the blue heat of his eyes.

Tension crackled between them.

"Do you think you'll do it again?"

Uninvited, but conjured up by his husky-voiced question, she pictured the two of them. Naked. Wet. Steamy. Aroused. She could never wear those pearls in the shower again without him being a part of it, just as he had earlier today.

She wrapped the strand around her finger, freeing it from his grasp. "No. I won't be doing it again."

He shoved his hands in his pockets. "I left my jacket yesterday."

His jacket. He'd come for his jacket.

"It's still in the kitchen. I'll be right back." She turned.

Behind her, Luke crossed the threshold. She whirled and stilled him with her hand. His heart thudded beneath her palm. Touching him was a mistake. She jerked her hand back.

"Don't come into the kitchen. Stay there. And don't close the door behind you." She was far too close to being naked on a countertop or slamming the door shut for a replay of the other night or dragging him into her shower to indulge in subtlety or good manners.

She hurried down the hall to the kitchen. Luke's jacket lay in a heap by the island. Olivia indulged in a few seconds of deep breathing. It was ridiculous that Luke's mere presence evoked responses beyond her usual range of emotions. One last deep breath and she was ready. Ready to take control, to prove she could maintain cool, calm, and collected with Luke.

She picked his jacket off the floor, noticing a smear of pale pink lipstick against the black leather collar. She rubbed at it with her finger, but it didn't budge.

She started back through the kitchen door, calling out to Luke, "I'm afraid I got lipstick on your collar—"

She stopped in midsentence, horrified to find Marion Turner, a fellow literacy committee member and gossip extraordinaire, framed in the open doorway. Olivia's stomach heaved. It had nothing to do with the rum punch and everything to do with the contemptuous judgment on Marion's face.

"Hello, Olivia. I'm sure I would've knocked, but the door was wide open. I was just dropping off the report for next week. It never occurred to me you wouldn't be dressed yet. But I can see—" her knowing look bounced from Olivia's semidressed state to Luke and back again "—you're busy."

Luke caught Olivia's eye and held her gaze for a few seconds. His calm nonchalance curiously calmed her.

Olivia pasted on a smile, determined not to look caught or guilty. She hadn't done anything. Not today anyway. "No, I wasn't busy at all. Do you know Luke Rutledge? He's starting our new library wing tomorrow." Olivia thrust the jacket toward him. "And he's just leaving."

"I just got here." Luke intoned at the same time.

"I remember Luke. He failed my English class. Twice." Marion's voice echoed her look of distinct disapproval. "And did he just get here or is he leaving? Never mind. Give me a call, Olivia, when you're not busy." She emanated disdain.

The old, familiar rush of inferiority threatened to swamp her.

Luke nodded his head with an arrogance that matched Marion's disapproval. "And it was a pleasure seeing you again, Mrs. Turner."

Marion sniffed. "Just remember if you lay down with dogs, Olivia, you get up with fleas."

Olivia saw Luke's slight flinch and felt it as if it were her own. Protective indignation quickly displaced insecurities. She might not like Luke, but she wasn't going to stand around while Marion took unwarranted potshots at him.

"It takes a flea to know a flea." Wait a minute, that wasn't right.

"I mean it takes a dog to know a dog. And it's lie. Lie down. Not lay." Comebacks were not her forte.

"Well, I never," Marion sniffed. "I trust you'll be dressed the next time I see you, Olivia."

How dare this woman insult her and Luke while standing in her home? "And I trust you'll have found your manners, Marion."

Marion whirled in a flash of green polyester and huffed down the sidewalk.

Olivia stood torn between laughter and exasperation. "I'm so sorry, Luke. She had no right to say that."

He shrugged, but she sensed her defense pleased him. "Let it go." The rigid set of his shoulders contradicted his words.

Quite frankly she was a bit shaken by the ugly side of Marion she'd just witnessed. "Why did she fail you?"

"I did a book report on *Zen and the Art of Motorcycle Maintenance*. She said Robert Persig was a pervert and she flunked me."

She'd experienced Marion's narrow range of literary acceptability firsthand. "I'm not a fan of his, but he's not a pervert. Anyway, she said you failed twice."

"She decided I could make it up by doing another book report."

"And?"

"*Fear and Loathing in America*. Hunter S. Thompson. She tried to get me expelled."

"You could've just read something on the list." While Marion's attitude and actions were reprehensible, this was the very thing about Luke she inherently found maddening.

"No. I couldn't." Luke shook his head slowly, an odd smile on his face.

Olivia tried to understand, but for a girl who'd spent a lifetime trying to fit in, she just didn't get it. "Why do you go out of your way to antagonize?"

"Why do you go out of your way to conform to everyone's expectations?"

"Privilege offers the opportunity to fly in the face of convention. When all's said and done, you still have your family's name to fall back on."

"So do you, Olivia."

"You're right I do. One misstep. One wrong move and I prove to everyone I'm the white trash they thought I was."

His blue eyes peered past the woman with the well-tailored clothes and elegant little house to glimpse the girl who'd endured the other children's thoughtless taunts when her mother abandoned their family. The child who heard the whispers about her father's drinking, the patronizing air of her "betters."

"No one can make you feel less than you are, unless you allow them to." His voice was soft and quiet, his touch tender as he tucked a few straggling hairs beneath her towel turban.

She'd never meant for him to see so much. Know so much. Some waters ran too deep and true to course to navigate. She shifted nervously to one foot. "You should go now. People will talk."

She didn't want to feel the stares, hear the whispers when she shopped in the grocery store.

"With Marion Turner, that's a given." He made no move to leave.

"So, you should go now."

"Come ride with me."

They held opposing views on fundamental issues. She didn't quite like him. She certainly didn't trust him. And the depth of emotion he stirred in her, quite frankly, terrified her. Despite that, an underlying note of need in his voice touched her.

"What?"

"On my motorcycle."

"Now?"

Luke laughed aloud at her. "Yes. On my motorcycle. Now. I suppose you could put on some clothes if you really had to."

"I couldn't..."

"Fine. Leave the clothes off." His voice dropped to an evocative, husky note, shifting them to a different plane of intimacy.

"I mean I couldn't ride with you." For one crazy moment regret lingered against her tongue like a bitter fruit. In that instant she longed to feel the heady rush of wind against her face, the throb of the powerful motor and the power and control in Luke's lean body as she held on to him. "I go out to my father's every Sunday. I tidy up and cook for him. I like to make sure he has a real meal at least once a week."

"Fine. I'll take you over to your dad's then we'll swing by River Oaks and you can pick up your car."

"But..."

"Are you afraid of what Marion and the other upstanding citizens might whisper behind your back?" His tone shifted from scathing to bracing. "Don't give them that much power over you, Olivia."

Something horrifyingly akin to pity flashed across his face. She preferred denigration to pity any day. How dare he pity her?

"Perhaps you could move past that monumental ego of yours and figure out I don't want to go with you. Period."

"Sugar, it doesn't have a thing to do with my ego. You loved riding that bike yesterday. You need your car back. You plan to go out to your dad's and I wouldn't mind seeing Bennett."

Momentarily distracted by his comment about her father, Olivia strayed off the conversational course. "Why would you want to see my father?"

Luke's gaze pierced her. "Because I wouldn't be where I am today if it wasn't for your daddy."

Olivia's eyebrows shot up, intrigued despite herself. "That's scary."

"I flunked out of my freshman year at college. I was studying banking so I could follow in the Colonel's footsteps." No surprise there on either count. "That summer I wound up on a construction crew your daddy supervised." Luke's mouth quirked in a rueful smile. "I was full of bad attitude."

"Some things never change," she teased.

He grimaced with self-deprecation and her heart did a funny little flip-flop. "I mean serious bad attitude. The Colonel was coming down hard on me for flunking out and besmirching the family name. I didn't want to be on that construction crew. I sure as hell didn't want to go back to school. Your daddy put up with me and my attitude for about half a day." Luke laughed and shook his head as if he could still see the fireworks. "My ass was grass and he was the lawn mower. Once he'd adjusted my attitude, Bennett taught me a lot. For the first time in my life, I discovered I was good at something other than raising hell."

She recalled his "Born to Raise Hell" tattoo with vivid clarity. It'd been one of the first things she'd spotted when she'd put on her glasses while he sprawled naked in her bed. Best not to think about him naked in her bed. Anyway, he'd given her plenty of other things to think about.

Her father a mentor? Bennett Cooper? The man she'd grown up with? Olivia was stunned. "He never mentioned you. But then again he spent most of his off time at the bar or in jail." She couldn't quell the lingering rancor. "The odd times he was home, our family wasn't enjoying Cleaver moments around the dinner table."

Luke shrugged. "We didn't have any of those either. While my father hammered home what a disappointment I was, your dad kept pushing me—pushing me to go back to school and get an engineering degree."

"I didn't know you had a degree. I thought you just owned your company."

"Does it make a difference? Yeah. Civil engineering from Virginia Tech."

"I never knew...."

"Why would you?" Luke shifted his broad shoulders. "Anyway, I'd like to stop off and see Bennett. Catch up with him." His voice lowered. "Say you'll come with me, Olivia. Don't let them hold you hostage with their opinion."

Olivia wavered, swayed by the hint of vulnerability she'd glimpsed beneath Luke's customary swagger and the measure of pity underlying his words as if she was pathetic in her concern with public opinion. And then there was a hint of a challenge. He fully expected her to turn him down. He thought she was so predictable.

"Give me ten minutes to get dressed."

A slow smile replaced his initial register of shock. Luke smiled with his whole face, his eyes crinkling at the corner. Ha. She'd got him.

She hurried down the short hall to her bedroom, the heat of his gaze warming her backside. And frontside. And inside.

"Let me know if you need any help dressing. Or undressing. I'm best at the last, but I'm available for either."

She closed the bedroom door and leaned against the hard panel, not at all sure she hadn't just made a tremendous mistake agreeing to go with him. His suggestive comment should have irritated her. Instead, she flushed, attuned to the play of nubby terrycloth against her sensitized skin. Yes, she remembered all too well, he was *very* good at the undressing part.

HE MIGHT'VE MADE a mistake. Luke, not a man given to second-guessing himself, second-guessed. He hadn't counted on how pushing Olivia would push himself. Right now he was hard pressed not to knock on her door and repeat his offer to play ladies' maid. His fingers itched to slide across her skin, slip beneath the cotton of her robe. Then he'd lower his head and tease his tongue against—

"Hi." A perky voice shattered his fantasy. "I'm Beth. Olivia's friend. I don't know if you remember me. I used to be Beth Harbison, but now I'm Beth Lamont." She shoved a finger bearing a wedding band in his general direction. "We were in high school together, but you were a few years older than me. Your brother Adam was in my graduating class. My hair was brown then," she gestured toward her flaming red hair. "But I've just decided to run with the red. It's hard to cover red, ya know. You probably don't remember me." She finally ran out of steam.

"Sure, I remember you." Nice, but a little ditzy.

"Oh. Well. How've you been?" She hopped from foot to foot.

One too many cups of coffee this morning for Beth, he guessed. "Fine. How about you?"

"Good. Good. I live just a few houses over." She pointed over her left shoulder. "So," she glanced around the empty entranceway, "where is she?"

He knew better, he really did, but it was just too plum an opportunity to pass up. "Liv's getting dressed."

Beth, formerly Harbison and now Lamont, almost bugged her eyes out of her head. "Really? She wasn't dressed? I'll just see if she needs any help." She shot down the hall like a launched rocket.

She darted into the bedroom. Once again, Luke stood in the hallway alone. What the hell? He nudged the new, unpainted door closed with the toe of his boot. Olivia had her chaperone and he was tired of drop-ins. He should've shut the door before Marion Turner had blown in like an ill wind.

Luke leaned against the doorjamb and picked up a book from the stack on the foyer table. *Pride and Prejudice*. Somehow that didn't surprise him. Luke replaced the book and picked up one of the two unopened puzzles sharing the tabletop. *Twice as challenging,* the box proclaimed. Each puzzle piece was double printed with two different views of the same subject. Clever. What you thought would fit on one side, might belong on the other.

He studied a black-and-white framed print on the wall. Damn. That was Olivia in the photo, caught in mid-air with a parachute strapped to her back. She was like that double-sided puzzle. Sometimes her pieces didn't fit on a side he expected. Just now, for example, she'd floored him when she took Marion to task on his behalf.

How long had it been since someone had taken up for him, championed him before censure? His mother, when he was still a small child, perhaps. Olivia was like no woman he'd met before. Despite the fact she didn't like him and Marion's opinion obviously mattered to her, she'd jumped in to protect him.

The fat cat appeared in the den doorway and blinked at him. Muted female voices traveled down the hallway. The cat—what had Olivia called it—strolled over and arched up on its two back legs, bumping its head against his knee. Luke hunkered down and scratched the thick fur behind its ears. He caught his name a time or two from behind the closed door. He grinned at the cat who merely slitted its eyes in kitty contentment. "Fat Cat—" he might as well call it that "—Beth's giving her the third degree. She's not going to be happy."

In a moment of blinding insight, he realized how important her happiness had become to him in just a day. As if cued by his thoughts, the bedroom door opened. Olivia marched down the hall, Beth trailing behind her.

Luke stood up slowly and looked at Olivia. A thick braid hung heavy over one shoulder. A long-sleeved T-shirt with a V neck hung loose on her except where she'd tucked it into well-worn jeans. She was classy and elegant and he had no business wanting her the way he did. But a hunger that had nothing to do with a want for food clenched low in his gut. "You're beautiful."

He hadn't meant to speak aloud. Actually he wasn't even aware he had until soft color washed Olivia's throat and face. "Uh, thank you."

"It's time for me to go," Beth piped up. Damn. He'd forgotten all about Beth.

Olivia seemed to have that effect on him.

"Let me grab a jacket and we'll all go out at once," Olivia said, a hint of panic on her face. She was a smart woman, his Olivia, if she didn't trust him alone. Because right now he'd love to fill his hands with her denim-clad cheeks while he kissed her as senseless as she made him. She'd definitely have to order another new door if Beth left them alone.

"Here." He stepped forward and wrapped her in his jacket. He rested the backs of his fingers against the shirt's soft cotton and an expanse of her silky skin. Her heart pounded wildly against his touch. His own heart thudded a response. Her eyes, huge behind her glasses, darkened. Her delicate scent, as subtle and elusive as Olivia herself, tantalized him.

"I'll just be leaving now," Beth muttered as she sidled toward the door, bringing him back to reality.

Olivia stepped away from him and practically ran for the door. "We're right behind you."

Luke followed, somewhat mollified that Olivia appeared as shaken as he was.

Beth hurried across the front lawn. "Nice to see you again."

"I'm sure I'll see you soon," Luke called to her retreating figure.

"I doubt it." He heard Olivia's muttered comment.

Olivia strapped on the extra helmet and climbed up behind him. Luke turned on, then cranked the bike. He torqued halfway around until only inches and their helmets separated them.

"Yes? Do you have any last-minute instructions for the ride?" Her breath was warm against his face in the chill air.

"No. I wanted to tell you I love that color on you." He glanced down at the brushed cotton T-shirt beneath his jacket she wore. "It's exactly the same shade as your nipples."

8

OLIVIA BANGED THE POT into her father's kitchen sink with uncustomary vehemence, out of sorts with herself, Luke and life in general. She stared through the cracked windowpane out at the swaying trees. He was wrong for her. He stirred something deep inside her that was frightening. All the other men in her life—from a dating standpoint—had been reserved, conservative. There'd never, ever been anything that remotely bordered on a discussion of body parts—certainly nothing close to Luke's frank, sexual comments. With Luke there was no dancing around issues. She knew he wanted her in a powerful, primitive way. It was confusing—both frightening and empowering. Luke pushed her outside her zone.

And he'd definitely shown her father in a different light. In retrospect, she realized Pops had always encouraged her to pursue her degree. How many times had he grumbled that Marty needed to move on beyond the auto parts store? He'd pushed Tammy to specialize in something. She supposed in his own dysfunctional way, Pops was as nurturing as he knew how.

Now he and Luke were enjoying the midday sun on the sagging front porch. She'd noted the genuine regard with which Luke had greeted her father. There'd been no hint of patronization. Unlike Adam's visit. With Adam, she'd found herself ashamed of the small house with a repair list a mile long, painfully aware of the marked difference between River Oaks and the Cooper homestead. Perhaps because she'd read Adam's unspoken criticism.

She struggled to dredge up her animosity toward Luke. Her antipathy felt safe. She didn't want to admire him or respect him—to care about him. She wasn't naive enough to think she could ever simply like Luke. Placid, moderate emotions didn't exist between the two of them.

Olivia glanced over her shoulder at the shuffle of footsteps down the hallway. Tammy. Olivia wasn't sure if she was capable of dealing with her sister right now. She might as well suck it up, because she didn't have a choice.

Tammy strolled in, sporting a belly-baring halter top with a denim shirt thrown over it, low-slung jeans that looked uncomfortably tight, a navel ring, chunky soled shoes, two inches of dark roots beneath her bleached blond and a guarded, slightly sullen expression. "Hey, Olivia."

"Hi, Tammy." She loved her sister, but even from the time they were small children, they'd never connected. Being with Tammy was like spending time with a stranger you'd shared a room with growing up.

"When did you hook up with a hottie like Luke Rutledge? Aren't you dating his brother?" Tammy eyed her as if she couldn't quite believe her boring sister had "hooked up with a hottie."

"We're not...I haven't hooked up with Luke." Was that the appropriate terminology? "He wanted to visit with Pops and he offered me a ride." She realized with a start that Luke had claimed so much of her attention, she'd actually spared Adam very little thought. She wasn't quite sure how to handle the subject of her relationship with Adam.

"You rode that hog?"

"Hog?"

"The Harley. The motorcycle." Tammy appeared insultingly astonished, as if Olivia had sprouted a third eye in her forehead.

"It wasn't that big of a deal." Actually, it was much the same as anything associated with Luke—intense, exciting, overwhelming, arousing. But she wasn't about to discuss that with Tammy. "How's the nail business?" Tammy had graduated from the Academy of Cosmetology and Beautification in March and rented a spot at Harriet's Hair Hut.

The sullen expression returned in spades. "I might as well tell you. Earl and I have split up." So much for husband number three. "Now Harriet's yanking my spot at The Hut. Go ahead. Say 'I told you so.'"

Harriet was Earl's sister and Olivia wasn't surprised she hadn't taken the breakup well. Olivia *had* told her sister working with an in-law might prove tricky. Especially considering Tammy's track record in the commitment department. Had Tammy split with Earl over Tim? Not only was Tim Earl's best friend, he was also Earl's brother-in-law, Harriet's husband. Or he had been.

Olivia winced. "Tim?"

Tammy waved purple and gold two-inch acrylics and stared Olivia down. "Tim."

Olivia shook her head, unable to contain her disapproval. "Oh, Tammy. That really wasn't the wisest choice."

"I know. I'm not stupid. Sometimes I just make stupid choices. There's a difference you know." She toyed with her belly ring. "Could you for once try really hard not to be so damn judgmental? When I'm with Tim I can't think clear—nothing else matters. It's almost like magic. I don't expect you to understand that."

That was exactly how she felt around Luke. For one unsettling moment in time, she and Tammy shared a wavelength. "I do understand" slipped out before she considered the consequences.

"Well, welcome to the land of the imperfect living," Tammy drawled, speculation simmering just below her surface. "You sure you haven't hooked up with the hottie?" She stabbed her thumb over her shoulder, in the direction of the front porch.

Good lord, what had just come out of her mouth? Olivia panicked. "Nope. Nope. No hook-up here. You were just so eloquent." Olivia scrubbed at the cheese sauce dried on the bottom of the pan. "Is that how you felt with Earl, Allen and Jerry too?" Olivia was pretty sure Tammy's second husband had been Allen, but she couldn't swear to it. "And I don't mean that in a critical sense. I'm really interested."

Tammy pulled a clean cloth out of drawer and started drying the dishes. "Kind of. You know it was that way at first." Tammy shrugged with love-the-one-you're-with fatalism. "I think this time, Tim's the one."

"Maybe." Olivia refrained from voicing her doubt. Tammy had the staying power of used tape on a cold day. Obviously these attractions where one felt bemused and enchanted didn't lend themselves to solid, long-term relationships. Was that the way it had been between her mother and father? Too bad her mom hadn't figured it out before she had three kids to leave behind. Her heart and her head took note.

Tammy cocked her head to one side. "You ever thought about dying your hair red? I bet it'd look good."

What was it with the hair color? First Beth, now Tammy. Why was everyone determined to make her into something or someone she wasn't? "I am not dying my hair red."

"All right, already. No need to get snappy. It was just a suggestion." Tammy tossed her golden locks with dark roots. "I thought red looked more like a chick who'd ride on a Harley with a guy like Luke."

"You're absolutely right." A tremor of disappointment rippled through her. Of course, a wild, red-haired "chick" was exactly the woman for Luke. Conservative, four-eyed librarians weren't meant to rip about with the resident bad boy. Why did she feel disappointment at having it spelled out for her? She knew she wasn't the woman for him.

"Hmm." Tammy snapped her out of her reverie. Uh-oh. She recognized the gleam in Tammy's eyes, having seen it countless times before. Trouble. Tammy's man-alert radar was going off. "Well, if things don't work out with Tim, I might have to look Luke up. Doesn't he start on the library tomorrow?" She dropped Olivia a heavily mascaraed wink. "I might have to stop by and see my sister. Maybe we could double date with you and Adam. Luke would be right up my alley. That is, if the thing with Tim falls through."

Something green, ugly and perilously akin to jealousy reared not just its head but its entire body in Olivia. *And maybe I'll have to bitch slap you.* She stunned herself with her vehement reaction. It was as if her encounter with Luke had opened a Pandora's box of passion inside her. She struggled to contain her emotions. She had no claim on Luke. None whatsoever. Nor did she want any. However, it struck her as supremely warped if her sister wound up in bed with him. And in Tammy's vocabulary dating translated to sex. If she had to, she'd sacrifice herself on the familial altar. "Stop by, but Luke's off-limits. He's mine, whether he knows it or not."

Tammy, who changed her affections at the same rate the wind blew, didn't blink at Olivia's about-face. She threw up her hands, surrendering the subject. "Cool."

"Now that's the best news I've heard all day." Luke's lazy, sexy drawl wrapped around her from behind.

Dismayed, she pivoted in slow motion to face him. He stood framed in the doorway, laughter crinkling the corners of his eyes. But it was the flicker of fire in his blue eyes, a carnal familiarity that weakened her knees. Her fingers clutched at the familiar edge of the nicked countertop.

What had she gotten herself into? She'd wandered into quicksand and the more she struggled to get out, the deeper and faster she sank.

LUKE CROSSED the buckled linoleum. Olivia stood frozen in front of the sink. He stepped between her and her sister.

"The gentlemanly thing to do would be to leave and pretend you didn't hear that." Her laughter rang light and flirtatious, threaded with an undercurrent of steel. She cut her eyes frantically in Tammy's direction.

Tammy merely leaned against the counter as if she were settling in for the latest soap opera installment.

"You're right about that, honey. But then I've never suffered from that particular affliction." Luke slipped his arm around the indent of her waist. Even though she stiffened against him, she was careful not to pull away. For whatever reason, she was playing to Tammy's audience. Only an idiot or a misguided gentleman wouldn't take advantage. Luke was neither. He tugged her closer, absorbing her fragrance while she gazed up at him with a forced smile. "That's one of the things you like about me, isn't it, sugar?"

Her delicate little foot ground down on his instep with painful accuracy. "Just one of many things."

"Why don't you let Tammy finish up here and you can show me the barn?" He extricated his aching foot from beneath hers. If she had declared them an item, he damn well wanted in on it. Her last update had confirmed she despised him. Never a dull moment with Olivia.

"I'd love to, but I need to finish washing up the pots."

"Go ahead, Olivia, live a little. Trust me, the best view is in the loft." Tammy winked and hustled them to the door.

"What about Pops?" Olivia looked as if she were being forced to walk the plank.

Luke nudged her out the door and down the stoop. "He's napping on the front porch."

Chickens scattered as they followed a dirt dogpath through the overgrown yard to a barn in even more desperate need of repair than the house.

Olivia waited until they were out of earshot. "You weren't supposed to hear that."

She deserved to squirm for crushing his foot. "I've always known the best barn views were from the loft."

"Not that. You know..." She shoved her glasses up on her nose, a gesture he'd learned was a measure of her nervousness.

"What?" It was so much fun to tease her.

"You know very well what. You weren't supposed to hear me tell Tammy you were mine." The words rushed out.

Luke slowed their pace. Once they reached the barn,

which put them out of sight of Tammy's probing eyes, Olivia wouldn't waste any time putting distance between them. For good measure, he looped his arm over her shoulder, pulling her close to his side.

"Physical contact isn't necessary."

"Come on, honey. You don't want her to think you're averse to my touch, do you?" He toyed with the thick braid hanging over her shoulder. "Not after you told her I was yours. That has a nice ring to it."

"I got carried away."

The barn, once red based on the odd remaining paint flakes, loomed before them, barely standing on this side of dilapidation. One of the massive double doors stood ajar, hanging on by one hinge. They slipped inside.

"I like it when you get carried away. I don't believe I've ever had a woman stake a claim for me so boldly before."

The air stirred around them, musty with the smell of old hay and tools that had worked the earth and been returned with bits of soil clinging to them. From a darkened corner, a chicken squawked her protest at their arrival.

Olivia ducked from beneath his arm and stood just inside the door, captured in a shaft of sunlight slanting through a missing board. "You know good and well...Luke Rutledge, that I didn't mean it." She crossed her arms over her chest.

"Damn, woman. You are hell on my ego."

"You possess enough ego for you and a couple of other men as well." Olivia narrowed her eyes.

"You wound me."

"Uh-huh."

"So, why'd you say it if you didn't mean it? Why's it so important for your sister to think we're an item? What could possibly induce you to align your fair self with someone as reprehensible as me?"

"You don't understand my sister. She changes men as often as she does nail polish. She was interested in you." Olivia pressed a hand to her forehead and shook her head. "She even suggested double dating. You and her with me and Adam."

Maybe when hell froze over. "It might be a good time." He pushed her button.

Olivia's head snapped up and she planted her hands on her hips. "Never."

"Why not?" He wasn't interested in the least in Tammy, but he had the distinct impression Olivia was jealous. Of him. He rather liked the notion.

"In Tammy's book, dating means sex. They seem to go hand in hand for her." The light streaming in behind her picked out subtle shades of red in her dark brown hair.

"Ah." He saw, but did she?

"It seemed rather sordid if she slept with you after we..." She squirmed in obvious embarrassment. "Well, you know, after what happened." A gust of wind startled dust motes into a dance about her head.

"Did it ever occur to you that I wouldn't leap into bed with your sister after...you know?" He couldn't resist mocking her.

Her perplexed expression proclaimed it hadn't. "Most men find my sister appealing."

"Perhaps you've confused appealing with available. And I'm not most men." He stepped toward her, stung that she thought so little of him. "Do you know what I think, Lady Olivia?"

She retreated, shifting out of the sunbeam's path into the shadows. "No. And I don't want to know."

To hell with that. He didn't particularly like the picture she'd painted of him. Lady Olivia was about to face a few home truths. "First, let's clear one thing up. Your sister could table dance naked in front of me, and I wouldn't be interested. Got it?"

She nodded mutely. He didn't imagine the relief in her eyes.

"Good. Now here's the most important part." He was damn tired of this buffer of denial she kept throwing up. He stepped close enough to see his reflection in her dilated pupils. "It's not about sordid. You can't stand the thought of me touching her the way I've touched you."

"Don't be ridiculous." He recognized knee-jerk bravado when he saw it.

"It's not even close to ridiculous." He reached out and wound her braid around his hand, a rope of thick silk against his callused palm. Her pulse fluttered wildly at the base of her throat like a snared bird when he traced the shallow indent of her collarbone with the fingers of his other hand. His blood thundered a response. "Don't hide behind your convenient conventionality. At least have the guts to admit you can't bear the thought of sitting across from me at dinner and thinking I might touch her this way." He trailed his thumb along the downy soft of her neck, past the stubborn line of her chin.

Luke didn't know whether it was his taunting words or his touch that provoked it, but he saw the truth flash in her eyes. "Yes."

"Say it. Tell me."

She turned her head aside. "I can't bear the thought of you touching her that way." She faced him once again, his hand still wound in her hair, her head at a haughty angle despite her admission. "Are you satisfied?"

"Not by a long shot, but that'll do for now." He drew her closer. "I liked it when you staked your claim." She braced her palms against his chest to stop him. "It turned me on."

"Probably everything turns you on." She sounded more hopeful than disdainful.

"Being deliberately insulting isn't going to work, you know." He took one of her hands in his and slowly brought it to his mouth, kissing the fleshy pad of her palm. The air between them shifted and changed, like the motes of dust and hay swirling about. Did she feel the heavy thud of his heart beneath her other hand? "And just to clarify, everything about *you* turns me on."

Her pulse raced against his fingers where he grasped her wrist. "Does that line work with all your women?"

"I wouldn't know, since I've never used it before." He rubbed the velvety skin of her wrist.

"Luke..." Her faint protest lost its meaning as her other hand clutched at his shirt instead of pushing him away. Her eyes darkened to a smoky gray.

She might be the prim and proper librarian on the outside, but inside she was fire and passion. She liked it when he spoke candidly, whether she admitted it or not.

"You're confusing now with the other night...the costume...the mask."

Perhaps she'd deluded herself with that theory. He knew better. They were custom-made for one another. "Baby, it doesn't have jack to do with costumes and masks. Everyone wears a mask. It's knowing what's real beneath it that counts. Maybe you had to put on a mask to find the real you." His mouth was warm against her racing pulse. "Because this is real."

"Stop." Her hand, fisted in his shirt, trembled against his chest.

"The way your hair smells, the touch of your skin, the way you taste..." he probed the valley between two of her fingers with the tip of his tongue, her sharp intake of breath hissed in the quiet of the barn as want slammed his heart against his ribs "...all make me hot for you."

"Don't talk that way." Despite her protest, she didn't move away. "I don't want to hear it."

"Why not? Because it makes you all hot and bothered too? Because you like it too much?" He read the answer in her parted lips, the darkening of her eyes. "You could always kiss me to shut me up."

"Or I could walk out." It was an idle threat and they both knew it.

"Yeah. That too. But I think you'd rather kiss me. I know that sounds like a much better plan to me."

"You're not a man of few words, are you?" she teased wryly.

"Not with you. You seem to bring out the best in me." His comment held a measure of truth.

"That's a scary proposition." Her eyes sparkled in the dim light.

Her playfulness charmed him. "Proposition? Are you flirting with me, Lady Olivia?"

"Absolutely not." She shook her head. "You and your ego. I'm trying to shut you up."

"I've told you how to do that."

She slid her hands over his chest and up his shoulders. Her mouth hovered a breath away from his, so close he inhaled the faint scent of cinnamon. His gut clenched in anticipation. No mistaken identity, no rum punch, no simmering anger. Of her own free will, Olivia was about to kiss him.

"Oliviaaaaaa. Olivia, are you in there?" Adam's voice shattered the moment. In an instant, Olivia transformed from a provocative woman on the verge of making him a very happy man to a withdrawn, uptight shell.

What in the hell was Adam doing here?

"I THOUGHT THAT WAS your motorcycle out front. What are you doing here?" Adam bristled at Luke. He turned to Olivia before Luke had a chance to respond. "And what were you doing in the barn with him?"

"She was showing him our antique tractor." Tammy stepped around from behind Adam, her tone daring him to infer otherwise. "We keep it in here to protect it from the elements."

She shot Tammy a grateful look. Of course, Tammy's story would carry more weight if the barn itself didn't appear ready to succumb to the elements at any second.

"You never showed *me* your antique tractor." Petulance was not a pretty sight on the face of a grown man. And unfortunately for her state of mind, she'd shown Luke a lot of things Adam had never seen. Would never see.

Olivia waded knee-deep in the testosterone surging between Adam and Luke. Luke opened his mouth, the look on his face clearly spelling trouble. She poked him, subtly of course, in the ribs and jumped into the conversational fray, not trusting Luke not to throw out some outrageous answer.

"I didn't think you'd be interested in the tractor. Luke offered me a ride out and then I'm picking up my car. Why are you here?" She'd read somewhere that the best defense was a good offense.

"I tried you at home and when you weren't there, I knew you must be out here." Adam slung a casual, albeit proprietary, arm around her shoulders. "I wanted to check on my girl. You feeling better?" Adam looked down his nose at his older brother. "Thanks for taking care of her for me."

Once upon a time—two days ago to be exact—Olivia would've enjoyed Adam's attention. She would've reveled in his assumption that the two of them belonged together. Olivia wasn't sure whether she should pin it on a change in circumstances or a change in her, but now his arrogant possession aggravated her. And she wasn't the only one. Luke radiated tension like a palpable force.

"The pleasure was all mine," Luke drawled.

"No doubt," Adam countered.

Sacrificing tact for expediency, she shrugged off Adam's arm. She found herself oddly compelled to defend Luke in the face of Adam's derision. "He was quite the gentleman. But you seem confused that I need a keeper. No one has to take care of me—especially not on your behalf."

Beth may have been right about Adam. He certainly exuded patronizing arrogance today.

Adam quickly backpedaled. "You're absolutely right. Of course you're capable of taking care of yourself. Although my brother as a gentleman is hard to imagine."

At one time she'd have thought it something of a stretch as well, until she considered she'd practically begged—okay, forget practically, she *had* begged—Luke to have his wicked way with her while she was mildly—okay, okay, *very*—intoxicated. It was a perverse day when she had to defend Luke's honor not once, but twice, to maintain some semblance of conscience. "He was every inch the gentleman."

Her face burned at her poor choice of wording.

"Maybe I could give you lessons," Luke drawled the challenge.

"I imagine there's very little you could teach me," Adam threw back.

Kissing popped into Olivia's mind, but, mercifully, not

out of her mouth. Luke could teach Adam a whole lot about kissing because he was very, very good at it.

"Don't be too sure about that." Luke bared his teeth in a mocking grin. With his jaw darkened with a shadow of a beard and his hair hanging loose, he looked sexy and dangerous and her heart slammed against her ribs.

Adam ignored Luke's taunt and cupped Olivia's elbow. His touch didn't wreak the havoc Luke's did. Not even a pitter-patter. "If you're done here, let me take you to pick up your car and then we'll have dinner together." Adam clearly expected her to fall in with his plans.

Luke clasped her other arm. "I'm dropping her off at her car."

She caught Tammy's eye. "Gentlemen, thank you both for your kind offer, but my sister is taking me to pick up my car."

Olivia strolled around to the front of the house, flanked by Adam and Luke, while Tammy brought up the rear. Pops snoozed on the front porch, blissfully unaware of the circus unfolding around him.

She stopped between the Beemer and the Harley. "And as for tonight, I have plans."

"Plans? You've never had plans before."

She'd never had back-to-back orgasms with Luke before either.

"Guess you're out of luck, bro." Luke threw fuel on the fire.

Rather than looking at Olivia, Adam glanced around the farm with a hint of desperation. "Maybe tomorrow. I'll call you." He glared at Luke. "When we can have some privacy."

"Okay. That's fine." She'd be busy then as well.

"And I'll see you tomorrow morning." Luke's voice

slid down her spine, laden with innuendo, bringing to mind a much better way to start the day than with a cup of coffee. He made a construction visit sound like an early morning rendezvous. Or maybe her mind was just obsessed with sex these days.

"The ribbon-cutting ceremony is at nine." She sounded appropriately prim and proper.

"I'll be there at eight."

"I'll be there by eight-thirty," Adam joined in.

Luke captured her with his blue eyes. "Be prepared for some changes." His voice dropped. "It'll be noisy. Maybe dirty. Definitely messy. But I can guarantee you'll be satisfied when it's all over."

She swallowed hard. She was close to satisfaction and he'd only talked. "You'll know if I'm not."

"I don't doubt it for a minute."

Adam didn't move until Luke did.

"Sure I can't take you to your car?" Adam tried again.

Instead of finding his persistence flattering, it irritated her.

"Positive."

"Well, I'll call you."

"Goodbye, Adam. Luke."

She couldn't wait to see the backside of both of them and sort through this jumbled mess.

Luke's gaze swept her lazily. "Nice shirt. It's the same color as your...cheeks. Nice and rosy. See you tomorrow."

Horrible, horrible man. Teasing her, taunting her, turning her on....

9

OLIVIA PULLED INTO her driveway, mentally and emotionally spent. By the time she walked to her unpainted front door, Beth had hotfooted across her lawn. "Tell me everything," she panted as Olivia opened the door.

"I need a cup of tea. Do you want one as well?"

"I want the scoop. But I'll take a cup too."

Beth ploughed ahead to the kitchen and settled on a bar stool.

Olivia filled the kettle. For the first time, the black-and-red tile and industrial chrome appliances failed to cheer her. She waited until the stove's blue flame hissed beneath the kettle to start her saga.

Olivia measured out a blend of oolong and sassafras while she recapped her afternoon. She dropped the stainless-steel tea balls into sleek, ceramic mugs.

"When Tammy took me to River Oaks to pick up my car, she offered how-to advice on juggling two men at one time." Olivia sat on the other stool and propped her chin in her hand.

"Your sister's definitely the expert in that department. Did you take notes?"

"I don't need to take notes because I have no intention of juggling either one of them. I plan to break things off with Adam—although, he's pursuing me harder than he ever did before. There's nothing to juggle with Luke because there's nothing..." The kettle shrilled its protest.

Even inanimate objects refuted her denial. Olivia hopped up and poured boiling water into the mugs.

"Then what's the big deal with Tammy going after him?"

"Luke and Tammy? The idea is beyond repugnant."

"Does that mean gross?"

"Close enough." Olivia paced in front of the sink.

"But why? No one knows except for you and Luke. And you yourself said it was a mistake and there's nothing there. You know what I think?"

"No. But let me guess—you're going to tell me." There seemed to be a lot of that going around today.

"Yep, I'm gonna tell you. You won't admit you want him, but you don't want anyone else to have him."

"That's not true." Was it? And why did Beth and Luke keep drawing the same conclusions?

"Listen, sister. I was in the same room with you two. I offered to leave because it was smoking hot. I don't think either one of you even knew I was there."

Merely thinking about Luke and his intense blue eyes sparked a flame low in her belly. "Okay. There's something there," she conceded, "but it scares me. I don't like feeling out of control. And Tammy's living proof that relationships based on physical attraction don't last."

"Tammy's living proof that she's desperate for someone to love her. She's just confused that physical love equates to emotional love." Beth dumped an obscene amount of sugar into her tea.

Emotional fragments shifted inside Olivia, straining to come together. "But, she..."

"What? You think she's just a sex maniac? Come on, Olivia. Your mother left and your father was hardly ever home sober. You looked for whatever it was you needed by taking care of everyone and everything. As long as everyone approves of you, all is right with your world."

Her world rocked on its axis. She'd never thought of herself or her sister in that context. Olivia shuddered at hearing herself described in such blunt, needy terms. "I sound so pathetic."

"You're far from pathetic. You compensate by giving. Tammy compensates by taking attention or affection from wherever she can find it. Tammy, who happens to be a little older, looked for love in all the wrong places. She still does. Look at the nails, the hair, the clothes, the belly button ring. She's like a little kid everyone ignores. Any attention, even if it's negative, is better than no attention."

"Oh." Tammy's words echoed in her head. *I'm not stupid. I just make stupid choices.* She toyed with the stainless-steel ball containing the spent tea leaves and stumbled through the thoughts swirling through her. "That makes sense—what motivates Tammy. But it doesn't change the fact that I don't want to make the same bad choices she does, based solely on a fleeting physical relationship."

Beth reached over and stilled Olivia's hand on the infuser. "That's getting on my nerves." Olivia put her hand in her lap. Beth continued, "Who's to say it's only physical attraction?"

"It couldn't be anything else. Adam is much more my type. Or at least he was. Adam and I share the same values. We want the same thing."

"And Luke doesn't?"

Their conversation after Marion Turner left had so clearly illustrated their differences. They viewed the world in totally different ways. "Luke's a law unto himself. I live according to society's mores. The only common ground we've found so far has been physical."

"You never know where it might lead. And if it doesn't lead anywhere, then you've had one heck of a good time. You know, chalk it up to one of those wild hairs you get occasionally."

Olivia scraped back her stool and gathered up the empty mugs. And what if he broke her heart in the process? Given the intensity that marked every exchange between them, it wouldn't be just a broken heart. It would be absolute devastation. Simply dating him would earmark her for gossip. An affair gone sour would shred her reputation. That didn't sound like such a good time to her. "I have to live here. This is my home and my work on the literacy council is important. My library programs are important. I refuse to jeopardize them for some fleeting chemical reaction." She rinsed out the cups in the sink. "And let's not forget, I slept with him under false circumstances."

"And it sure did feel good didn't it?" Beth emptied the tea leaves into the compost jar and turned to face Olivia. "If you could turn back time, would you go back and give up that against-the-door experience?"

LUKE SPREAD THE architectural plans for the Colther County Library expansion on his coffee table. Three weeks to complete the addition, three and a half tops. Then Olivia would remain in her new tower and he'd be off to middle Florida for a new project. Would she miss him when he left? Would she welcome him when he returned? Every time he took a step forward with her, he wound up two steps back.

He scowled as he heard a car approach. He owned a

couple of hundred acres at the end of a dirt road because he valued his solitude. No one just dropped by.

He left the plans on the table and crossed the room, his curtainless window offering a view of the front yard. Adam had parked his car and was walking toward the house. Luke could count on one hand—even missing a few fingers—the number of times his brother had stopped by. This was about the last damn thing he needed now.

He met Adam on the front porch, closing the door behind him. They could conduct whatever business Adam had—and there was an agenda, no doubt—on the front porch. "What's up?"

Adam shrugged as he mounted the stairs. "Just a brotherly visit." He settled into a rocking chair without an invitation.

For the life of him, he'd never understood why Adam couldn't just speak to the matter at hand. Hell no. Adam always danced around an issue—a little soft shoe shuffle and double-talk. "Visit away."

Luke fished out his knife, grabbed a piece of wood out of the pile he kept on the porch for whittling and dropped to the top step. May as well whittle while he waited for Adam's song and dance routine to warm up.

"Nice piece of property here."

"Yep. Usually it's nice and private."

Adam ignored his blatant reference and ploughed ahead. "Bennett Cooper owns a nice spread as well." Adam brushed at his creased jeans. "I didn't know ya'll were such friends."

"I check in on Bennett now and again."

"He's a drunk." Adam couldn't quite mask the sneer in his voice.

"Yep. So is Uncle Jack."

"You should help him."

Luke was deliberately obtuse. "Who? Jack?"

Adam's nostrils flared. "Uncle Jack's different. He doesn't wind up in jail."

Olivia's words that privilege afforded the freedom to disregard convention whispered in the wind swaying the green-needled pines. "I believe he can thank the Rutledge name and money for that."

"Jack's a social drinker." Adam refused to entertain the notion that a Rutledge might share common drinking problems with a plebeian Cooper. "But you should help Bennett. He's really got a problem."

"Does he beat his kids? Other men's kids? Does he destroy property?"

"You know he doesn't. But it's your civic duty."

"A man's got to make his own choices. If you mean I should preach to him, then I'll forego my civic duty." Wood chips flew from the point of his knife. "Bennett knows I'm his friend. If he ever needs help with anything, whether it's giving up booze or mowing his pasture, he knows he only has to call me."

"That's a big place for a man Bennett's age to keep up with." Ah, Adam was starting the soft shoe. Shuffle twice to the right.

"He seems to manage."

"For God's sake, the front door is held on with duct tape," Adam proclaimed, as if Bennett had violated a sacred code of home ownership.

Luke grinned at Adam's outrage. "That's just Bennett. He could be thirty years younger and living across the hall from you at River Oaks and he'd probably duct tape his door."

Adam visibly blanched at the prospect.

"You've got to look beneath the duct tape and the Wild Turkey to the heart of the man. Can you do that?"

"I have. And I'm worried about Bennett. Just like I'm concerned that Olivia runs herself ragged taking care of her family."

Yeah, right. Adam was concerned about Adam. And if it somehow affected him, he was concerned.

Luke shifted until his back was braced against the porch post. Olivia was a lot of things—exasperating, exhilarating, enchanting, stubborn as hell, but she was no one's martyr. "That's her choice."

"Duty and obligation seldom leave *some of us* a choice. It's one of the things Olivia and I have in common."

Adam lent new meaning to supercilious. And he could damn well leave the martyr shtick at home or try it out on someone else.

"Damn, bro, I've been confused for a long time. I thought you lived at home because you have a staff to cook and clean for you and wash your car and the house is so big you have absolute privacy. And then there's the free-rent factor." Luke shook his head in mocking admiration. "Instead, I discover you've spent years chained to River Oaks, bound by duty and obligation to a mother who heads the Garden Club, the Ladies' Auxiliary, the Fine Arts Committee and walks about five miles a day and a father who manages to squeeze in at least five rounds of golf a week, both of whom are waited on hand and foot by the same staff that serves you. Glad you cleared that up for me."

Adam scowled. "You make me sound like a parasite. I'm speaking to the Rotarians on Monday, you know."

Ah, there was some logic. Apparently parasites weren't allowed to address the Rotarians. And yes, he did know, since his warm, caring, brother had allowed someone else to accompany his sick girlfriend rather than risk germ exposure and blow his Rotarian appearance.

"Hmm." He'd learned a long time ago it was often best to not fully engage his family in conversation.

"So, I've been concerned about both Olivia and Bennett."

"Civic duty?"

"It's much more personal than that."

Luke ached to share just how *personal* he'd been with Olivia and wipe that smug look right off Adam's face, but he'd promised Olivia.

"Yes. And because I care for both of them, I've worked out a plan that I feel suits everyone's needs."

Translation: Adam's needs. He couldn't wait to hear how deep this shit was about to get.

"Really? Well, let's hear it."

"If I buy Bennett's property, we can relocate him to a house in town, something closer to Olivia. I'll invest the funds for him, manage his portfolio and he'll never have another worry for the rest of his days."

Which would number few because Bennett would croak if he was taken off his land.

"And you'd be willing to do that for them?"

"Olivia is *special* to me."

Yeah, her father had property Adam desperately wanted. "How special?"

Adam stood, hopefully to take his leave. Luke snapped his pocketknife closed and hauled himself to his feet as well.

"She's very special. Would you be willing to sort of soften Bennett up? You know, put in a good word for the plan? Maybe you could introduce the idea of selling. Do you think you could talk to him in the next day or two?"

"No problem." The more Adam regarded him as an accomplice, the more he would find out.

"Great." Adam sauntered down the steps, turning at the edge of the grass. "By the way, I saw the way you looked at Olivia earlier today." Adam chuckled and shook his head. "Forget about it."

With that one comment, Adam slid beneath his skin. "Give me one good reason why I should."

"Because I can offer Olivia the one thing you never can—the thing she values more than anything else." Adam opened his car door and braced one loafered foot on the floorboard. "Respectability."

Adam got in the car, throwing him a mocking salute.

Luke kept his face impassive. Luke couldn't offer her respectability, that much was true. He'd ruined his reputation years ago. But brother Adam shouldn't be so arrogantly sure that respectability was the most important thing to Olivia.

As Adam's car disappeared in a cloud of dust down his dirt road, he glanced down at the wood in his hand. He held a rough, miniature replica of a mask.

OLIVIA DOUBLE-CHECKED the concealer caked beneath her eyes. Hmm. Dark circles magnified by her glasses, further accentuated by the library's fluorescent lighting. Beth's question, "Would you give up that against-the-door experience?" had nagged her. The memories it provoked had tormented her. One sleepless night and she looked liked death warmed over. Mercifully ground-breaking ceremony photos didn't involve closeups.

Her assistant, Cindy, poked her head around the bathroom door.

"The newspaper photographer's here. We're still

waiting on some of the chamber members and Mrs. Turner from the Literacy Committee."

"Thanks for letting me know."

Cindy shuffled from foot to foot, her florid complexion turning redder yet. "And, uh, Mr. Rutledge—the one with the construction company—told me to tell you to quit hiding in the bathroom."

Olivia bit back a distinctly un-librarian-like, four-letter word. Rather than share with Cindy where a particular Mr. Rutledge could put his jackhammer, she pasted on what she hoped was a civil smile. "I'll be out in just a minute."

Luke. He kept her up at night and tormented her during the day. It would be a shame if after six years of college and a degree she lost her mind—she didn't want to even consider her heart—to Luke. And her job. And her position on the committee.

She'd reached three conclusions during her restless night. One, she wouldn't give up that against-the-door experience, even if she could turn back the clock. It had been incredible. There. She admitted it. And she had a new door, sofa and mattress to boot.

Second conclusion. There wouldn't be any more against-the-door experiences. Something powerful blazed between her and Luke, but those things didn't have any lasting power. And the immediate gratification wasn't worth the ultimate cost. An affair with Luke could destroy her socially and emotionally. It was rather like skydiving. She'd done it once and survived. She wasn't willing to take the risk again.

So, she'd remain civil. And distant. If she could just keep him from talking to her she'd be fine. It was when he started talking that she got in trouble....

Third conclusion. She had to extricate herself from her relationship with Adam.

Olivia left the bathroom and approached the group gathered by the front door. Somewhere in the midst of her conclusions and resolutions, she'd obviously over-looked passing the message along to her senses, which shifted to red alert. She felt Luke's presence before she spotted him, as if she'd entered some private magnetic field. The low murmur of his voice drew her. Even in the crowd, she perceived the scent particular to him.

The group shifted and her heart trip-hammered. This was a new side of Luke. He looked every inch the suc-cessful owner of a construction firm. A stonewashed denim shirt—the sleeves rolled up to expose bare, sexy hair-sprinkled, tanned forearms—was tucked into khaki work pants. His thick-soled work boots were worn, but polished to a high shine. His hair was pulled back neatly with a leather strip, throwing his features into harsh re-lief. Everything about him was hard and lean. Despite the air of success, an untamed element clung to him.

Beside him, Adam appeared slightly paunchy and fussy, with everything from his hair down to his khakis starched to the nth degree. Did he starch his boxers as well?

Adam caught her eye on the end of her ungracious thought. A guilty blush stained her face. Adam left the small group and hurried across the carpeted floor to greet her. Olivia noted the slightest pause as he checked his reflection in the glass separating the reference room from the main library.

"How's my girl this morning?" Adam's hearty tone and possessive attitude scraped on her sleep-deprived nerves.

"I have no idea. But I'm fine." Olivia countered her irritability with a smile.

"I missed having dinner with you last night." Adam moued his mouth into a pout of disappointment. A pouting man was patently unattractive. "Did you enjoy your *plans?*"

"They were fine." Washing her hair had proved uneventful.

"Why don't I treat you to dinner out tomorrow night?" Adam offered.

Olivia, not particularly up to speed on the intricacies of the male-female relationship, finally caught a clue. Brushing Adam off wasn't going to work. The more unavailable she made herself, the more intently he pursued her.

"Okay."

Undaunted by her lack of enthusiasm, Adam beamed. "I thought something nice and romantic, maybe Cristo's."

Cristo's, an hour's drive away, constituted serious wining and dining. "The Steak and Shake is fine."

"Not for you. Not for tomorrow night. For the next week, Cristo's is testing a dining theme. In the spirit of a dinner theatre, their patrons are to dine in disguise. I thought we could wear our costumes since I missed the party Friday night." Adam preened. "I rather fancy myself as a swashbuckling pirate."

Panic nearly blinded Olivia. That pirate's costume again. Could she sit across the table from Adam, with him wearing what Luke had that night…? Olivia drew a calming breath. Of course she could. No big deal. It was dinner. And really, what did it matter whether they wore costumes? She'd tell him she couldn't see him any more over dinner.

"That sounds fine."

Luke walked up as the last words left her mouth. He bent at the waist in a sweeping bow, his eyes alight with devilment. "Good morning, Lady Olivia." His mocking voice slid down her spine.

Her stomach flip-flopped. What streak of perversity deep inside her found him so physically appealing she could barely catch her breath?

"Hello, Luke."

"Ready to start work? Olivia and I were just planning dinner out tomorrow night in our costumes, since she missed me in my pirate outfit."

The twinkle in Luke's eyes disappeared. "That should gather a crowd at the Steak and Shake."

"Cristo's." Adam dropped a wink at Luke. "Only the best for my girl."

"Once you've had a taste of the best, it's hard to settle for less. Isn't that right, Liv?" Luke's eyes glittered, his face hard and mocking.

His words evoked a barrage of erotic sensory memories. The exquisite pillage of his tongue deep in her mouth. The salty flavor of his essence. The velvet warmth of his mouth and tongue against the back of her neck.

Her blood rushed on a mad course of desire at a pace and to places it had no business rushing in the middle of a Monday morning in the Colther County Library in the midst of a crowd.

Marion Turner's arrival saved Olivia from responding to Luke's provocative comment. Despite their exchange yesterday, Olivia could've kissed her. "Marion's here. We can move forward with the groundbreaking now."

She preferred a cool reception from Marion to Luke's hot tension and Adam's romantic tenacity.

The sun shone brightly despite the brisk bite in the air as the photographer hustled them outside and shuffled the group around.

"Tallest on the back row. That's it." With a harried expression and his camera dangling from a strap around his neck, the photographer lined up his back row.

A tremor of excitement shook Olivia. They were one step away from starting the new addition to the library. A year of lobbying, months of fund-raising and it was about to happen. She wanted to shout and indulge in a few steps of an Irish jig. Instead, she mentally wrapped her arms around her happiness.

Luke glanced at her across the shuffling group. Time stood still. The corners of his lips curled in the faintest of smiles as he nodded his head, sharing her joy as surely as if she'd announced it. Olivia smiled back, as if it was the most natural thing in the world, sharing this unspoken connection with him. Startled, Olivia caught herself. It was one thing to feel the flow of sexual energy between them. It was terrifying to sense an even deeper bond.

"Okay. The rest of you fill in on the front." The photographer caught her arm, pulling her front and center. "You're the librarian, right? Okay, let's get the chamber president and the builder down here."

He placed Adam to her left and Luke to her right. Someone handed her a shovel.

"Right-o. On the count of three, everyone say cheese."

10

"EASY. This truck looks bad enough already." Dave, his dispossessed partner, leaned against the hood, as Luke tossed a defective two-by-four into the truck bed.

He was in a helluva mood and not particularly good company for anyone. At least Adam had finally left to work on his Rotarian speech or whatever it was he did behind his respectable desk inside the respectable bank their respectable family owned.

"Don't you have anything better to do with a day off?" Luke checked off the last of the supplies. Only a few problems out of the whole shipment—not bad.

"Thought I'd check out what prompted a last-minute schedule change. You know this was my project, pal." Dave pulled a bagel out of a bag. "Bagel? Just got a shipment." The scent of garlic wafted across to Luke. You could take the man out of New York, but you couldn't take New York out of the man. Dave's family shipped him fresh bagels three days a week. Dave smeared on cream cheese. "And don't tell me you yanked the project to be near your family, 'cause that dog won't hunt."

Dave had made a hobby of collecting and using, on a regular basis, every Southern colloquialism known to man. Most of the time, Luke enjoyed the way Dave's brogue twisted around the phrases he'd grown up on. Today it wasn't so amusing. What the hell was Olivia thinking, going out to dinner with Adam?

He grabbed a doughy bagel out of the bag and didn't bother to answer.

"Could it be..." Dave looked past Luke's shoulder, a flirtatious smile on his face. "Well, if it isn't my favorite librarian. I'm going to pretend it's my incredible charm that draws you out and not garlic with a double order of lox."

Olivia smiled at Dave as if she'd discovered a long-lost friend. She damn sure never looked at Luke that way. No, she eyed Luke like she'd just caught a glimpse of the bogeyman.

"When I heard you wouldn't be on the project, I hoped you'd at least stop by." She reached for the white, wax-paper bag, and grinned. "With your bagels."

Luke's bite stuck in his throat. He swallowed the lump. "Dave's engaged." It came out bald, blunt and unadorned.

Olivia pushed her glasses up onto the bridge of her nose and speared him with a reproving look. "Cynthia. I've seen her picture. She's quite lovely."

"Just wanted to make sure you knew." Luke snatched up the plans. "Now some of us have work to do."

He did have work to do and it was a damn sight better than standing around watching the mutual admiration society at work while he made an even bigger jackass of himself.

Dave laughed and called out as Luke stalked around the corner, "I'll look you up before I leave."

Luke bit back yet another surly comment. Every man he knew seemed eminently acceptable to Her Highness. Except for him. Luke approached the flatbed truck and pitched in unloading the supplies that hadn't fit on a pallet. Nothing like back-breaking physical activity to put things in perspective. Unfortunately, physical activity brought to mind rumpled sheets and Olivia beneath him. And on top of him. And beside him. Warm and naked, her hair loose, tangled about her bare shoulders, her pearls wrapped around one succulent—

"Make sure you don't strain something," Dave instructed from behind him.

Luke straightened and left the crew to finish up. "Through already?"

Dave grinned, not the least bit daunted by Luke's abruptness. "Man, you've got it bad."

"Take a hike, Klegman."

"I wouldn't have believed it if I hadn't seen it with my own two eyes. The mighty hell-raisin' Lucas Jasper Rutledge has succumbed." Dave appeared to be thoroughly enjoying himself. He chuckled all the way back to Luke's pickup.

"I thought Olivia might have something to do with the sudden change of plans. Quite a switch from your usual bar babe."

"I hate to shoot your theory to hell, but Lady Olivia has an aversion to me."

"I'd say she had something for you, but I wouldn't call it an aversion. But then again, you didn't see her eyeing your sorry excuse of a butt when you stomped off."

Luke crossed his arms over his chest, even more annoyed by that news. She eyed his butt and made out with him, but still planned dinner out with Adam? "Yeah, well, I'm not some piece of meat, ya know."

Dave threw back his head and laughed. "God, you sound like a woman."

He was losing his mind. Olivia was driving him crazy. He pushed his hard hat back and grinned sheepishly. "Yeah, I guess I do."

"Have you tried wooing her?"

For one crazy moment, Luke thought he said screwing her. That hadn't worked. Maybe that was the problem. They'd skipped the wooing and gone straight to screwing.

"I can see by that dumbfounded look on your face, that hasn't occurred to you, Romeo. Get with the program."

"Who are you, The Love Doctor?"

"Might I remind you which one of us is happily engaged to the woman of his dreams and which one of us is Mr. Only Lonely with a bad attitude?"

Dave had a point. A smart-aleck point, but a point nonetheless. "You have my undivided attention."

"What seems to be the problem?"

"She's dating my brother."

"So, she's had a little lapse in judgment. Show her the way. You're dealing with a woman of substance."

Luke looked past the row of trees lining the parking lot. "She's too classy for me. She always has been."

"That's where you're wrong. I'd say she's just what you need. And don't sell yourself short. You've got something she needs—and not necessarily what you're thinking. There's fire brewing beneath her cool exterior and I think you're just the man to stoke the flame."

A van with Carson's Floral Delivery detailed on its side panel pulled into the parking lot. A kid who barely looked old enough to drive got out and went around to the back, pulling out a crystal vase filled with roses and little white flowers.

"Someone's got roses."

Why the hell did Dave feel obligated to state the obvious? "Looks that way."

The kid walked past them on the sidewalk and

hoisted the vase in a salute. "Take note, gentlemen. The ladies love this. A dozen red roses and she's putty in your hands."

Smart-ass kid.

"Maybe those are for me," Dave quipped.

The kid smirked. "You don't look like Olivia Cooper to me." He didn't break stride as he headed to the front door.

"Maybe next time, huh?" Dave turned to Luke, indicating the flowers with his head. "Her family probably sent them."

"Yeah. And maybe there really is a Santa Claus. It would never occur to her family." With Bennett, it'd more likely be a quart of Wild Turkey so he could offer to drink it for his teetotaling daughter. "Nah. It's Adam." His scum-sucking, lowlife, respectable brother.

"A dozen roses." Dave whistled. "He's pulled out some big guns there, partner." Dave laid a considering finger alongside his nose. "But, then again, it's fairly cliché. You need to come up with something original. Something that speaks to *her*." Dave raised his brows, "Think you're up to it?"

Luke had just the thing in mind. "No problem. My gun's much bigger than his."

OLIVIA SAT PROPPED on a bar stool in her kitchen, relieved to be home. Alone. No, really she was. She was ecstatic her day was over at the library. Thank goodness she wouldn't look up and see Luke watching her or catch a glimpse of him working side by side with his men. She wouldn't catch a note of his voice and flush at the sound. No glimpse of him in a hard hat to render her weak-kneed. No lingering scent particular to him to tease her hormones into a frenzy.

At least not until tomorrow morning.

She pushed off the stool and went to the back door, gazing through the window at the wine-red roses on the patio table. Too bad she was highly allergic. She could've sworn she'd mentioned that to Adam. Apparently her allergy had slipped his mind. Mentioning it when he'd called to make sure the flowers arrived would've been rude.

Dinner at Cristo's. A dozen long-stemmed roses. Three brief days ago—which felt more like a lifetime— she would've been floating on a cloud. Well, at least she'd have been pretty darned happy. Now she fought off a panic attack. Guilt had to be the culprit. Between now and tomorrow night she needed to come up with a polite, forceful, diplomatic way to dump Adam.

Easier said than done. She sipped a mouthful of tepid tea and reached for a notepad and pen.

I don't think we're right for one another. Forget it. She'd never convince Adam he wasn't right for her. Cross that off.

I want to see someone else. Ditto on the he'd-never-believe-it thing and in a town this small, she'd have to stage a public fling or Adam would know within days she wasn't seeing anyone else. And Olivia didn't fling in public. No go.

Let's just be friends. Strike three. It'd probably make him more determined than ever. She nibbled on the end of her pen.

I've taken a vow of chastity. Nah.

I'm frigid. Don't go there.

You're too good for me. Bingo. That wouldn't be such a hard sell for Adam. She underlined it twice and circled it.

The doorbell rang. It couldn't be Beth. Beth would

come to the back door. And if it wasn't Beth, she really didn't want to talk to anyone else. She could pretend not to be home, but the car in the driveway was something of a giveaway. Perhaps they'd simply go away.

The bell chimed again, killing that theory. A nice, polite knock followed. What if it was some sweet little Girl Scout standing on her front porch, gathering her courage to pitch thin mints and tagalongs? What if she, Olivia, was missing out on s'moas and trefoils because she wouldn't rouse herself and answer the doorbell?

She catapulted off the stool, hurried through to the front door and threw it open. Luke.

"You're not a Girl Scout."

"You're right."

He only had to stand there and her body responded. She needed serious help. "I bet you were never even a Boy Scout, were you?"

"For a day. I got kicked out." His voice lowered to a beguiling caress. "Let me in and I'll tell you why."

Olivia blocked the door, her breath in her throat and her knees in a less than steady state. Rationale and reason, ousted by lust and lasciviousness, flew out the window when he was around. "I don't want to know why."

"Okay. I won't tell. But I have something for you."

For the first time she noticed he held a professionally wrapped—expensively wrapped—package.

She unobtrusively pinched the back of her thigh. Ouch! Yeah, she was awake. This was real.

"Come on, Liv, let me in. There's nothing to be afraid of." Her nipples tingled and tightened in response to his low, husky urging. Easy enough for him to say. She'd acquired a voice-activated libido with Luke that frightened her almost as much as it excited her.

The rigid thrust of her nipples against her silk blouse

caught and held his attention. His confident demeanor shifted slightly. The deep breath he drew gave him away.

Power surged through her. Testing the waters of her feminine wiles, she ran the tip of her tongue along her upper lip. His hands holding the package trembled. Turning him on was turning her on. It was heady, exhilarating. Something wild and reckless inside her rose to the surface.

She stood aside. "Come in." Where was her better judgment when she needed it?

"Where do you want it?"

Muscles deep inside her body clenched in anticipation. "Where would you like to give it to me?"

"Your choice."

Olivia led him to the den. Every nerve in her body seemed tuned to him. Each breath seemed to be filled with him, his scent, his presence. Stepping through the doorway, Luke's arm brushed against her shoulder blade. Even that minimal contact sent a shiver down her spine and notched up the heat low in her belly.

Olivia skirted a stack of books and sat on the couch. Instead of following, Luke positioned himself behind the sofa. She looked at him over her shoulder. "I don't bite."

His gaze raked over her, the heat in his eyes searing her. With slow deliberation, he leaned forward until his breath mingled with hers. "I can't guarantee that I won't."

He placed the package in her lap. It was heavier than she'd thought, and thick. The backs of his fingers pressed against her thighs, stirring a longing so intense she shook. Luke continued to lean over her, bracing his arms against the back of the couch. "Go ahead. Open it."

His warm breath stirred wisps of hair that had escaped her chignon against her nape.

She ran her fingernail beneath the edge of the paper, loathe to rip into the elegant wrapping. She preferred to take her time and savor the anticipation. Tension radiated from Luke. She bit back a tiny smile. Was he nervous? She was. What would an unpredictable, sensual man like Luke give a woman like her?

She folded back first one edge of the paper, then the other. A set of sheets. Not pima cotton. Not percale. Not flannel. Silk. Apricot silk sheets. Sensuous, luxurious, decadent silk. "I love them," she breathed.

"I hope the color's okay. It's one of my favorites." His lips almost brushed the shell of her ear.

It was the same color as the shirt she'd worn yesterday. The same color as her nipples, according to Luke. She turned her head to look at him. His overwhelming maleness made her ache. "They're beautiful." Her voice rasped.

His heavy-lidded glance caressed her aching tips. "Yes, they are."

She meant the sheets. He obviously meant her breasts. His mouth hovered mere inches away. Unbidden, she recalled the sensation of those firm lips suckling her.

She swallowed convulsively. "You didn't have to do this, but thank you." No way should she accept such an intensely personal gift from him, and no way was she letting them go.

"I owed you a set of sheets." Luke reached down to her lap, his thumb brushing against one puckered nipple on the way. His brief touch arrowed to her womb. He pulled out a pillowcase, his thumb once again flicking against her nipple.

"Feel it." He gentled the material against her neck.

Olivia closed her eyes and dropped her head to the back of the sofa. She gave herself over to the sensation of silk sliding against her neck. The male scent particular to Luke mingled with cherry tobacco further aroused her.

"Mmm," she moaned her appreciation.

Luke deliberately released the pillowcase. It slithered between her breasts, puddling against her thighs. "I looked at a lot of sheets. I touched a lot of sheets. But these felt like you."

He hadn't picked up the phone and ordered flowers she was allergic to. He'd thought about his gift and taken the time to shop and paid attention to detail.

Trembling, she stood and walked to the door, but paused to look over her shoulder. "Would you help me put them on the bed?" She shushed the voice of reason vetoing the invitation.

"I'm here to do your bidding." He followed her down the short hall to her bedroom.

"All that arrogance at my command?" Daylight had given way to dusk, leaving the room shadowed. She turned the bedside lamp on low. Light spilled onto the comforter and pooled on the wood floor.

"I believe you've misinterpreted my gentle, humble nature."

She walked around to the other side of the bed, laughing. "And I believe you left that behind with diapers."

"Let me prove myself. I'm under your control."

There was a heady thought. How did he manage to be devastatingly sexy and fun at the same time? "Okay. Go ahead and strip..." she paused wickedly "...the sheets off the bed."

His teeth gleamed white against the shadow of a beard darkening his jaw. "My pleasure. I'll be very good. Why don't you sit and watch?"

Olivia sank into the wingback chair in the corner of her room. "Whenever you're ready."

Luke draped the comforter over the footboard and started on her sheets. Who in her right mind would ever find anything sexy in watching a man take sheets off a bed? Which just went to prove she wasn't in her right mind.

Grasping the top hem in one hand, he wrapped the pale cotton around his dark, hair-sprinkled wrist. Legs spread, his powerful thighs braced, he tugged and coaxed until it fluttered to him. He gazed across the bed at Olivia as he deliberately brought the sheet to his face and inhaled. "It smells like you."

"Oh." She wasn't capable of saying anything more.

"I would recognize your scent anywhere, Liv. I love the fragrance of you." He rubbed the fabric against his cheek, then released it to pool at his feet.

She moistened her lips and stroked the velvet chair arm, grateful for its support.

Olivia stared, fascinated, as Luke slid one finger beneath the elastic and eased it over the edge. The muscles in his arms and shoulders rippled as he leaned across the bed and rimmed the sheet free with one finger.

Watching Luke strip her bed brought to mind his deliberate, clever hands tugging off her skirt, his fingers slipping beneath the edge of her satin panties.

He tossed the last sheet to the floor. Her movements as calculated as his, Olivia pulled the pins from her hair, freeing it to tumble about her shoulders.

Luke's eyes darkened in appreciation. "I've wanted to do that all day."

"It gets in the way if I leave it down at work. And it doesn't look very professional."

"Hmm." His gaze devoured her across the bed. "No,

it doesn't look professional at all. It's very soft. Very sensual. Definitely too sexy for work." He gestured to the sheetless mattress. "Now that I've stripped for you, don't tell me I have to do the next part by myself as well. It's so much more fun together."

She rose and crossed to the bed. "I wouldn't dream of asking you to make it alone."

"We should start with the bottom." Luke tossed the sheet onto the middle of the bed.

Olivia fondled the sheet, smoothing the silk with the palm of her hand. She cupped her hand over the rigid, rounded corner, coaxing the fabric into place. Luke mimicked her sensual movements. Only one of Luke's corners remained.

"I may have to stretch it a bit, but it should fit."

Olivia wet her lips as he drew the fabric over the edge. His hand caressed the smooth surface. "Nice and tight. It's a little more work, but worth it in the end. I prefer a tight fit, don't you?"

"Absolutely." Her muscles clenched in agreement.

"Feel it now, Olivia. Soft and smooth. Supple, yet tight. Go ahead. I want to watch your face while you touch it."

Closing her eyes intensified the sensation as she fingered the fine fabric—nowhere near as fine as the texture of Luke's skin, but still exquisite. The sueded silk was just as he'd described. Her lips parted and she sighed her pleasure. Luke's harsh breathing whispered across the expanse of apricot silk.

She opened her eyes and rubbed her hand across the bed one last time, nearly touching his thigh. "I love the way it feels." And, for the moment, she loved the way he made her feel—like some wild, hedonistic creature.

"I knew you would. You're a very sensual woman, Olivia." He embraced her with his voice and his eyes.

She pulled out the other sheet, savoring the rich weave against her fingertips. "Now for the one on top."

"It spreads so much easier on top. Just lift and tuck it in." The memory of him on top, before Adam's phone call, hung between them as they inserted the bottom and smoothed the fabric up the bed with long, lingering strokes.

"Last, but not least, the pillows." Luke picked one up and kneaded it in his big, broad hands. "You have very nice pillows, Lady Olivia. Plump and full, yet soft." Her breath came in ragged pants. Her against the door. Him inside her. His hands clutching her buttocks, kneading them in much the same way. "You've got a very nice pair of pillows. Just the kind I like."

He slid the case on and reached for the other pillow. Once again, he massaged the fullness as he slid the case on. He propped them against the headboard and smoothed the comforter into place.

"I think you're ready."

She was beyond ready. Olivia was so hot, she wouldn't have been surprised if the sheets burst into flames from the heat coming off her body. "I appreciate all your help." She placed her palms flat on the bed and leaned forward, deliberately displaying her breasts to him. "How can I thank you for such a thoughtful present?"

Luke braced one knee against the edge of the mattress and leaned across to meet her in the middle. He buried his fingers in her hair and pulled her mouth to his. "Think of me when you're in bed naked tonight." His lips were hard and hot as his tongue plunged into her mouth. She met it eagerly with her own. Abruptly he released her. "'Cause I'll sure as hell be thinking about you."

By the time Olivia recovered her senses, Luke had closed the front door behind him on his way out.

11

SURELY AT SOME POINT in his thirty-two years, Luke had faced something more difficult than walking away from Olivia. However, nothing immediately came to mind. It was nearly impossible to think past the sweet taste of her mouth and his hard-on. It had required every ounce of self-control and self-discipline to remember his vow to court her and not jump her bones. Especially when her bones seemed more than willing to be jumped. This wooing business was damn hard on a man. But he was determined to prove his worth to Olivia and he'd forego one night for a future together.

He rolled down the pickup window as he left the lights of town behind him. Bracing cold air rushed into the cab, the next best thing to a cold shower. He pulled out a small cigar from the pack on his seat and lit it.

He slowed his truck, but at the last moment bypassed the road leading home. The yawning emptiness and solitude of his house didn't appeal to him. He was so keyed up, he'd only pace the floor. Cecil's? Nah. He wasn't up to shooting the bull with the boys over darts and drafts.

Acres of rolling farmland flanked the ribbon of blacktop. The lights of an occasional house and his truck punctuated the otherwise dark canvas of land and highway. Three-quarters of a mile ahead the road intersected the newly opened highway extension. His lights picked out a rusted mailbox, the hinged front missing. Luke braked and turned onto the Cooper property. Even from here, he could see the television's glow through the window. Bennett was up. No time like the present to let his old friend in on what was going on. He just hoped Bennett was sober enough to understand.

OLIVIA READ THE SAME PAGE for the fourth time, still clueless as to what it said. She relegated the book to her nightstand and turned off the lamp. There had never been a time when she couldn't lose herself between the pages of a good book. Until tonight.

She shifted, the caress of the sheets against her bare skin feeding her restlessness. She checked the bedside clock. Again. Almost eleven. Late. At this rate, she'd never sleep.

Luke's presence lingered in her room, in her bed. Each brush of the sheet against her body became his deft hand. She tasted him against her tongue. She smelled him against the plump, down-filled pillows beneath her head. Her bedside phone beckoned.

She rolled over and faced the other direction. It was late. Too late for a phone call. But she really should thank him again. And perhaps if she called he'd offer an explanation as to why he left so abruptly.

Actions that would never withstand rationale in the light of day often found credence in the hours between late night and early morning. Olivia twisted and reached for the phone, then hesitated. She should throw on a nightgown or at least a T-shirt and panties, shouldn't she? She'd never made a phone call in the buff. It seemed indecent. Wickedly naughty. She licked suddenly dry lips, her heart racing. It was a phone—not a video camera. He'd never know.

She drew a deep breath, turned on the light, picked up

the phone, and called information. A computerized voice relayed his number. She piled her pillows against the headboard, tucked the sheet around her, and dialed.

Ring. Just a quick thank-you.

Ring. Give him a chance to explain.

Ring. She should hang up....

"Hello?" he answered, his voice low, a little lazy, as if she'd stirred him from the verge of sleep. She could still hang up and he'd be none the wiser. "Hello?"

She clutched the phone, closed her eyes and took the plunge. "Luke. It's Olivia." Too late now. "Is this a bad time? I, uh, know it's late. Were you still awake? I can let you go." She sounded like an idiot. She should've written down what she wanted to say instead of babbling.

"Yes. No. I mean it's fine." He sounded rattled as well, not his usual cocky self. "Is everything okay?"

"Everything's fine. I just wanted to say thanks again for the sheets. They're lovely."

"You're a lovely woman, Liv. You deserve nice things."

Since she'd known him, he'd been provocative, seductive in the things he'd said to her. But that was the sweetest, most tender thing anyone had ever said to her. No one had ever called her lovely and no one had ever offered the opinion that she might merit more than the basic creature comforts. Tears gathered behind her eyelids, one sliding down her cheek, as emotion clogged her throat. "Oh, Luke..."

"Baby, are you crying?" Luke's tenderness touched her.

"No." A sniffle betrayed her shaky denial.

"Oh, sugar, I never meant to make you cry." He crooned low in her ear.

While she was making all kinds of a late-night fool of

herself, she might as well dredge up the question that had haunted her for years. "Luke, do you remember kissing me behind the bleachers at a high school football game?" All the air whooshed out of her lungs.

"Like it was yesterday." No teasing note contradicted his sincerity.

"Why did you kiss me?" She clutched a handful of sheet. She'd waited thirteen years to ask the question.

He didn't hesitate. "Because I wanted to."

She needed more of an answer than that. She screwed up her courage and forged ahead. "But why did you want to? Was it a bet? Because you thought I'd be easy?"

"Give both of us a little credit." She imagined him shaking his head. "You were the last girl on the easy list and I'd have kicked anyone's butt who'd tried to make a bet on you. I'd noticed you before." He sighed into the line. "I saw you when you left. I only meant to offer you comfort. But you were so lovely, and when I touched you..."

She still recalled the tremor of awareness, the first bloom of her sexuality, when his hands cupped her shoulders.

"...it was as if..." he hesitated "...as if I'd found a part of myself in you."

She couldn't deny a connection as well. "But you never said anything to me afterwards."

"You took off as if the hounds of hell were after you."

"You terrified me." And still did, to some measure. He tapped into a part of her and took her places inside herself she wasn't sure she wanted to go. He tapped into the wildness inside her that she'd always managed to control and subdue, except for periodic outbursts.

"That was pretty clear. And you've been straightforward as to where I stand with you since then."

"Luke?"

"Liv?"

"I don't hate you." She couldn't apologize for saying it, because at the time, she'd meant it and he'd deserved it. She couldn't offer him more, because, quite frankly, she didn't know how she felt about him. He was nemesis, champion, tormentor, lover—all rolled in one.

"That's good to know." His voice held a note of wry acceptance, as if he knew that was the best she could offer. "I didn't want to leave tonight, Liv." His voice strummed through her body. "I've thought about you all night. I can't sleep for thinking about you." His low, caressing tone didn't sound as if he found her repugnant. "Have you been thinking about me?"

She snuggled into the down of the pillow. "Yes. I've been thinking about you."

"You're not in the kitchen sipping tea, are you?"

She traced a circle on the sheet with her nail and smiled. "No. I'm not in the kitchen."

"You're not curled up on the couch with a book and Fat Cat are you?"

Despite his teasing tone, she knew the road they were headed down. Her heartbeat raced, even as she laughed softly, "It's Hortense. And no, I'm not on the couch, either."

"Are you in bed?" A hoarse note replaced his banter.

She paused. "Yes." Breathless embarrassment tinged her single reply.

"Oh, baby." He sucked in a harsh breath. "Do you want to talk for a while?"

They both knew where his "talk" would take them. She knew what he was asking. Did she have the courage? Anticipation sizzled through her. "I think I'd like that."

"Why don't you tell me what you're wearing?"

"Nothing. I'm not wearing anything." He groaned on the other end. "I haven't put you to sleep, have I?" Did that hoarse voice really belong to her?

"Not yet. I think I can manage to stay awake for another few minutes." She imagined his sexy grin.

"What about you, Luke? Are you in bed? Are you naked?"

"Yes."

A wave of lust crashed over her, through her, at his one-word response. Luke naked presented a spectacular sight. "You have an unfair advantage. You've seen my bed. Describe yours."

"Lonely."

Her breath caught and her heart ached at his stark description. "Come get in bed with me. I'm lifting the sheet. Do you want to slide in between them?" The words came without thought. She lifted the edge of the bedcover. Her own bed had been lonely far too long.

"Lift a little higher so I can slip in. Ah, you feel so good, Liv."

"I'm glad you're here." She imagined the brush of his hair-roughened thigh against her hip, the width of his shoulders and the span of his chest as they blocked the light. "Are you...excited?"

"Excited's the watered-down version. Try aching." She was. "Throbbing." That too, deep inside. "What about you, Olivia? Are you excited?"

Did birds fly south in winter? "Yes."

"Do your breasts ache?"

Luke made her feel, both emotionally and physically, things she'd never felt before. Instinctively, she seemed to know what he craved from her as well. "Yes. For your touch."

"Are you throbbing between your legs?"

Her entire body felt afire. Her muscles contracted within her as if he'd stroked her with his finger instead of a question. "Yes, for you."

"I want to see your beautiful breasts. Will you show them to me? Pull the sheet down. That's it, nice and slow. Let it slide over your sensitive, aching tips."

The silk dragged against her hardened nipples. Her breath quickened to short, sharp pants. "Ohhh."

She closed her eyes and imagined him beside her.

"Are the sheets the same color as your nipples? Look at yourself. Tell me."

She glanced down, as he'd requested. Her bare breasts against the material was an arousing, erotic sight. The tension inside her wound tighter. "They're a shade lighter, but very, very close."

"I want you to touch your breasts now. Taste them." Her nipples tightened to turgid points. "You'll have to do that for me."

She filled her hands with her breasts, the phone on her shoulder. "They feel heavy." Her eyes fluttered shut and it was Luke's hands that cupped her.

"Yes. Luscious Ripe," he murmured. "Put your fingers in your mouth and wet them." She held the phone close to her mouth as she laved and suckled her fingertips, trusting the line to carry the faint sounds.

Luke groaned on the other end. "Now roll your nipples between your thumb and forefinger." His command was harsh. Arousing.

She followed his instructions and bucked into the air and back against the mattress as sensation arrowed through her. "Ohhh."

"That's it, baby. Tug. Harder." The rough edge of his voice urged her on.

Fever gripped her. Sensation rampaged her. She released the pebbled tip. She knew he was aroused. She longed to touch him. "I want to hold you in my hand. Stroke you. Will you do it for me?"

Strain hoarsened his voice. "I don't think that's a very good idea, honey. I'd like to stay with you until the end."

He deserved a little teasing for leaving her high and far from dry earlier. "But you are still hard?"

He choked on the other end. "Yes. I'm still at full attention." He paused. "Liv, I love the feel of your skin, the way you smell. Rub your hand over your belly for me."

She slid her hand over her stomach, her belly quivering, muscles clenching at her touch. She saw herself, her body and her sensuality, through his eyes. She moaned into the phone.

"Baby, you're better than any fantasy I ever had. Rub your hands over your thighs. I love your thighs. Soft. Round. Smooth."

Olivia skimmed her hands over her thighs, her skin ultrasensitive to the slightest touch. His pleasure and her pleasure tangled into one despite the distance separating them.

Luke's voice rasped low in her ear, "Your hands are on your thighs, aren't they?"

"Yes." Muscles contracted against her fingertips.

"Bend your knees now and spread your legs for me." His harsh breathing echoed in her ear and with her eyes closed, he was there beside her.

She dropped her legs open. Exposed. Vulnerable. Powerful. "They're spread. For you."

"You're so beautiful. I can see you naked on those silk sheets with your legs open. You're wet, aren't you?"

The curls brushing against the back of her fingers were drenched. "Yes."

"I'm going to touch you now. Do you want me to touch you?"

Want surged through her, clenched deep inside her.

"Yes." She cupped her wet mound. In a state of near delirium, Olivia could almost believe it was Luke.

"Go ahead. Touch yourself. That's it. Are your lips swollen and slick?"

Sensation arched through her body, her nerve endings so sensitive her pleasure bordered on pain. "Yes." A whimper bloomed in the back of her throat.

"Baby, I can't hold on much longer. I want to hear you say my name when you come."

Luke's voice faded, becoming one with the stimulation that overwhelmed her. She chanted his name in an orgasmic litany as she spasmed to a point beyond mere pleasure.

Luke's groan on the other end penetrated as she regained coherence. "Oh, Liv, that was incredible. You're incredible."

Her essence perfumed the room. She tugged the sheet up over her spent body.

Cold reality began to edge out blinding passion. "Thank you." Was that the appropriate thing to say to the man you'd just shared mind-blowing phone sex with? She couldn't quite believe she'd just done what she'd just done except she had that sated after-sex lethargy and Luke's seductive voice in her ear.

"I'm glad you called, Liv."

"Sure. Maybe we can do it again soon." Dear God, her mouth and her brain had disconnected—possibly short-circuited by sex.

"Anytime. Don't lose my number."

She'd better get off the phone before she said some-thing else consummately, supremely stupid. "Good night, Luke."

"'Night, Liv. Sweet dreams."

Olivia hung up the phone and buried her face in her pillow. Her emotions might be a jumbled mess, but her head clearly recognized the dangers inherent in any kind of relationship with Luke. Moderation—which had marked her life, her decisions, her emotions—flew out the window when she was with him. He brought out the wildness she'd fought so hard to control and subdue all her life.

She had to stop this madness with Luke.

IF HE HADN'T BEEN abundantly clear that he and Olivia had shared an extraordinary experience via the phone line last night, Luke might've thought he'd fantasized it. All morning she'd politely, distantly avoided him like the plague. He'd tried to talk to her when she'd finished up the ten o'clock toddler story time. Instead she'd hus-tled off to handle a checkout, claiming her assistant needed a break. Sooner or later, she'd have to talk to him.

Olivia, chatting with her assistant, had her back to Luke. If she didn't see him coming, she couldn't run.

Luke approached quietly.

"Cristo's? Wow. That's a pretty swanky place." Her assistant was impressed.

Olivia couldn't possibly think she was going to keep that date now. Not after last night.

"I need to leave early. Can you close for me tonight?" Even now her voice turned him on—until what she'd said sunk in. Incredulity gave way to searing anger.

"Excuse me, Ms. Cooper. Could I see you in your office? We seem to have a problem." Without giving her a chance to do more than blink, he took her by the arm and hustled her to her office, leaving her assistant somewhat dumbfounded.

Olivia eyed him as if he'd lost his mind—and indeed he felt very close to it. She spoke over her shoulder, "I'll just be a minute, Cindy."

"Hold her calls," Luke barked and slammed her office door behind him. A framed print skewed drunkenly on the wall. The leaves of a tall, potted plant swayed.

Chest heaving, gray eyes shooting fire behind her glasses, she stood toe-to-toe with him. "What in the hell do you think you're doing?" She bit off each word and flung it at him.

"No, honey, what in the hell do *you* think you're doing? Over my dead body are you going out with Adam." He knew he was behaving like a heavy-handed jerk.

"Then prepare to die, Mr. Macho, because I'm going." She shoved her glasses up onto her nose. "Not that it's any of your business."

"None of my business?" She could make a production about her sister being off-limits, but he was supposed to stand around like some eunuch while she went out with Adam? They were about to get on the same damn wavelength. "I believe I gained a vested interest the first time I came inside you."

Defiance and denial flickered across her face. "That doesn't count. It was a case of mistaken identity."

Her answer further infuriated him. He took a step forward, backing her against the edge of the wooden desk. She needed contact with reality and he knew just the man to give it to her. "But you did know who I was last night, didn't you sweetheart, when we *talked* on the phone? There wasn't any confusion that it was me when you were writhing and moaning on the sheets I gave you, was there?"

The memory of last night slipped into the anger pulsing between them. Naked skin. Mutual cries of satisfaction.

Her chest rose and fell. She moistened her lips with her tongue. Even in the midst of anger, his gut tightened in response. "That was a mistake. I should've never called. Next time I'll send a note."

That's why she'd frozen him with the cold shoulder all morning? One of the most potent sexual experiences he'd ever had and she referred to it as a mistake. He was damn tired of her reducing everything about them to mistake status.

Luke struck back. "If your notes are as interesting as your phone calls, I'll look forward to it. You're teaching me so many new things—doors, sheets, phone calls." She was like a potent drug and the more he had of her, the more he craved her.

Frustrated with her and equally frustrated by his response to her, he crossed his arms over his chest and leaned back against the closed door. "But you are not going out with Adam."

She planted her hands on her hips, her breasts jutting beneath her blouse. "I don't take orders or ultimatums."

Luke reeled himself back from the tempting thrust of her chest to the matter at hand. "So, it's tacky for me to go out with your sister, but I'm supposed to sit back like Mr. Wimpy while Adam wines and dines you?"

"Did it ever occur to you, you testosterone-laden moron, that I'm trying to break it off with him?" She shoved her glasses up and narrowed her eyes. "And I didn't know you were so eager to go out with my sister."

"Dammit, I'm not. I just don't understand how it's different."

"Let me spell it out for you. *S-E-X*. Dating Tammy means sleeping with Tammy. Going to dinner with Adam means going to dinner."

"Yeah? Well, much like your sister having a different agenda, I don't think Adam's just looking for dinner." He'd been spinning so out of control, he hadn't really listened to her earlier comment. "You want to break things off with Adam?"

"That's what I said. I told you that Friday night, after…after I discovered I'd made a mistake."

"Oh." Adam wouldn't take no for an answer. It would be so easy to tell her now. *He wants your father's land. He's using you.* The words sat on the tip of his tongue but wouldn't come. He wanted her to make a choice independent of the land deal. And the knowledge was sure to hurt her. And the last thing he wanted to do was hurt the woman he loved.

The realization didn't floor him. Hell, he wasn't even surprised. In a way, he thought maybe he'd known thirteen years ago that there was something between them that very few people ever experienced.

She braced against the edge of her desk. "Oh? You act like a raving lunatic and all you can say is *oh?*"

He shoved away from the door. "You're right." He swallowed hard and forced out the words that didn't come easy. "I'm sorry, Liv. I kind of lost my mind at the thought of him touching you." He skimmed the soft satin of her cheek with his hand.

She swallowed convulsively. "Apology accepted."

Luke gentled the backs of his fingers against the delicate line of her collarbone. Her nipples stabbed against her silk blouse, in response. "I want you to tell Adam about us, Olivia."

"You promised you wouldn't—" Panic blanched her face.

He dropped his hands to his sides. "I promised I wouldn't say anything and I won't. You tell him, honey."

She wrapped her arms around her middle and looked away from him. "Isn't it enough that I won't see him again?"

"No, it's not enough. Tell him about us."

She faced him once again, her eyes filled with regret. "There is no us, Luke."

Luke had bared his soul to this woman last night. And now she'd taken the piece of him she'd always had and ground it beneath her heel. "Oh, I see. I'm just the dirty little secret tucked beneath your bed that you pull out when you need a little late-night phone sex."

"Luke, it's not that way—"

"No? Then why don't you explain how it is. Make me understand." Dammit, he wanted to understand. Desperately.

"I don't know how I feel. Everything's so confused in my head. You push me too far."

If she'd stop denying the part of her she'd suppressed so long, she might stop denying them. Woo her. Court her. "Go to dinner with me tomorrow night."

"A date?"

She looked as surprised as if he'd asked her to dance naked on top of the desk. That actually wasn't a bad idea. He shook his head to clear it. He was supposed to concentrate on the wooing, not the... "A date. You know, that thing where I pick you up. We go to a restaurant. Talk about the weather, books, movies, my job, your job. I bring you back home. A date."

"People would talk."

Ah, Olivia's golden egg of respectability.

"Yes. They probably would." Luke wasn't a man of half measures. If he wanted something, he went for it. If he believed in something, he stood behind it. It was time to lay it on the line. "I love you, Liv."

Panic flared in her gray eyes. "Don't confuse lust with love."

Luke smiled, more amused than offended. "I have shocking news for you, my sweet. I wasn't a virgin the other night." A blush crept along the ridges of her cheekbones and a flash of something satisfyingly akin to jealousy flashed in her eyes and tightened her lips. "I know all about physical lust. And it's true that you make me hard," he molded his hand against her skull, his thumb brushing against her temple, "just like I make you wet. That's physical lust and it's a powerful force between us." It shimmered between them now, drawing them closer, tightening his body to a throb. "But it's my soul that hungers for you."

Luke reached for the doorknob behind him. She had to make her own decision. "Give us a chance, Liv. Some people search a lifetime to find what we have."

Tears pooled in her lovely gray eyes, confusion and indecision marked her delicate features, but she offered him nothing in return.

12

OLIVIA STARED at the lady-in-waiting costume hanging on her closet door. Could she follow her original plan? Could she put on the dress, don the mask and go to dinner with Adam, hiding behind some trumped-up excuse for breaking up with him? She could, but she wouldn't have much respect for that woman.

She flopped back on her bed. This was all Luke's fault. How fitting he'd disguised himself as a pirate. He'd stormed her defenses, discovered a hidden part of her, and besieged her senses. He'd shaken her preconceived notions at their very foundations. He'd convinced her they could build on something more than a physical attraction.

She'd spent years denying—had gone to great lengths to bury—the wild passion Luke brought out in her. She'd always thought her passion meant she was like her mother and her sister. She had hidden behind the literacy council and her job and her reputation. How many years had she used other people's standards to measure her own sense of self-worth? For as long as she could remember. How much longer would she appoint others as the keepers of her self-esteem?

Luke loved her.

"Luke loves me," she spoke the words aloud to her empty room. They felt awkward against her tongue. She reached beneath the comforter and rubbed the sueded silk sheets, as if they represented a tangible measure of his feelings.

The notion nearly frightened her out of her mind. What if she dared to believe him? What if she opened her heart and her mind to his love? She'd tasted the depth of passion between them. Loving Luke, being loved by Luke, would be all-consuming. Could she open her heart to that kind of joy? That kind of hurt? She hadn't allowed herself that level of vulnerability since her mother had walked out the door.

Her heart mocked her head. *You foolish woman, as if you really have a choice.* Her head rejected her heart's chiding. Loving Luke Rutledge would prove downright inconvenient. She wanted a love that felt safe and warm and dependable, rather like slipping into a comfortable bathrobe at the end of the day. And while she did feel safe and warm with him, for the most part it was more along the lines of staring over the edge of a dizzying cliff.

Olivia hauled herself off the bed and crossed to her costume. She ran her finger over the material. Regardless of how much starch she'd sprayed on the pleats, they wouldn't conform to their initial stiffness. Luke had bamboozled, befuddled and bedeviled her to the point that whether she liked it or not—and she didn't—he'd insinuated himself in her heart.

Hortense padded into the bedroom. Olivia scooped her up and scratched beneath her chin. "You know that man that's been over the last few days? You know the one—dark, dangerous, sexy. What would you think if I was beginning to care for him?"

Hortense slitted her eyes.

"Hmm. Trouble. That's what I say too."

She stretched her neck, inviting Olivia to continue to

pamper her. Olivia settled her on her bed, earning a baleful glare. "Sorry, princess, I've got to take care of that trouble."

She couldn't—no, wouldn't—put on that dress. Her course of action was crystal clear. She checked the clock. Half an hour until Adam arrived.

She snatched up the phone with one hand and fished out the business card Luke had given her the morning he started the project with the other. She punched in his cell number. An odd calm descended upon her. He answered on the second ring. "Yeah?"

"Luke, it's Olivia."

"Yes?" His tone was guarded. Had he changed his mind? Did he regret their earlier conversation? There was only one way to know.

"I accept."

"I need a little more information to go on." Was that wary optimism on his end?

She sucked in a deep breath of courage. "That date? Our date. You know, where you pick me up. We go out for dinner. We talk about books, movies, your job, my job. You bring me back home. Perhaps you could walk me to the door. I have a new one you know." Joy cautiously bloomed inside her.

"People will talk." She heard the grin in his voice.

"I suppose they will." The thought unnerved her. "I'm going to tell Adam."

"What are you going to tell him?"

"About us." She plunged over the side of the emotional cliff she'd avoided since she'd met him.

"Say it again."

A tingle raced down her spine. There was something very sexy when he issued those directives over the phone.

"Us. You and me."

"Our date."

"Yes. Can you be at my house in twenty minutes?"

"Give me fifteen. I love you, Liv."

"I...like you a lot." It was the most she was capable of.

Faint laughter echoed on the other end as she hung up. Or perhaps it was her mocking heart.

"WRAP IT UP, Sam," Luke yelled to his job foreman. "I'm out of here for the day."

She liked him a lot. Luke grinned as he wheeled out of the library parking lot. That was a damn sight better than *I don't hate you.* Lady Olivia was coming around. He'd almost given up on her, unsure whether she could get past the rigid insecurities that held her prisoner to public opinion.

Luke prepared for battle as he drove. Adam, faced with losing Olivia and her father's land prospects, wouldn't be a happy camper. Luke, however, was ready. He'd made a few inquiries this afternoon, called in a few favors. The Rutledge name did carry a certain measure of power.

He sat impatiently through a second red light. Brother Adam and the Colonel had crossed the line between shady dealings and breaking the law. Luke had more than enough ammunition to win the battle *and* the war.

Luke pulled into her driveway and parked beside Adam. Adam climbed out of the Beemer, decked out in full pirate regalia. Good grief, if Liv had mistaken him for Adam, she could've only been barely mistaken.

Luke slammed his truck door behind him. "Evening, Captain Hook."

"Go home, Luke. You don't have any business here. Olivia and I have a date."

"I asked him to come, Adam." Olivia stepped out of the front door. "Come in, please."

Tension marked her smile and stiffened her shoulders. He met and held her eyes with his own. *You can do this, baby*, he sent her a silent message.

Adam marched up the sidewalk, scowling. "Where's your costume? Why aren't you dressed?" He glanced back over his shoulder at Luke. "What is going on?"

Luke followed at a more measured pace. Olivia was calling the shots on this one.

"We need to talk." She closed the door behind them. "Why don't we all sit down?"

"I prefer to stand if you don't mind." Adam assumed the pose of a swashbuckler, one arm on the mantel, a foot propped on the hearth. Brother Adam had watched one too many late-night flicks.

Luke settled on the couch. Olivia perched on the edge of one of the overstuffed chairs flanking the fireplace. Fat Cat eyed Adam and hissed. Luke knew he liked Fat Cat for a reason. Tension, thick enough to slice, hung in the air.

Adam frowned at Fat Cat and Olivia. "Now, what is the meaning of all this?"

Olivia wove her elegant fingers together and settled her clasped hands in her lap. "Adam, I can't see you anymore."

Adam momentarily forsook his Errol Flynn pose and gaped in surprise. Clearly, he hadn't expected that. "But...Olivia...darling...we're an item."

"There's something you should know." Her gaze flickered to Luke and then back to Adam.

"Whatever it is, it won't come between us," Adam assured her.

"I wouldn't count on that," Luke drawled from his vantage point on the sofa.

"When Luke brought me home from the masquerade party," Olivia paused and looked at the floor, rubbing her hand over her brow. She looked up again, shoulders squared, her head held high. "Luke and I were...intimate."

Her voice didn't betray how spectacular their intimacy had been.

Adam frowned, once again taken aback. "Intimate? How intimate?"

A blush stained her neck and face, but her head remained at a proud angle. God, he loved this woman. Once again, she glanced Luke's way. He silently nodded his encouragement. She shifted her attention back to Adam. "Very intimate."

Luke barely refrained from preening. Adam's expression of stunned disbelief was priceless. His "ice princess" had thawed for someone else.

"Did you know it was Luke?" He shoved the eyepatch onto his forehead.

She shifted in the chair. "No. But I...care...for him."

Adam turned to Luke. "You bastard. You knew how I felt about her. How could you?"

Luke clamped down on the urge to knock the hell out of Adam. Yeah, he knew how Adam felt about Olivia and ached to say it. Unfortunately, that would only wound her. "I wanted her."

And that didn't even begin to describe it. Even in the midst of confrontation, he hungered for her. A familiar ache settled in his belly. He glanced at Olivia. A response flashed in her gray eyes.

Adam eyed him with haughty disdain, anger simmering below the surface. "That's the way it's always been, hasn't it, Luke? It's all about you and what you want and to hell with how it affects everyone else."

An element of truth hit uncomfortably home. "I believe you're getting off the subject."

"No, brother, this is just a subject you'd rather not address. All these years you've thumbed your nose. Flunking out at school. Vandalizing public property. Coming home drunk. Did you ever once stop to think how that made Mother feel? Did it ever occur to you it might be humiliating for our entire family? Let's see, how did you put it once?" Adam pretended to ponder the question. "Oh yes, being true to yourself. I call it being a selfish bastard."

Olivia's face, so expressive and easy for Luke to read, reflected empathy. As if she related firsthand to Adam's scenario. Adam had just successfully sown powerful seeds of doubt in Olivia's heart.

Luke faced the ugly truth. His father had disowned him, his mother had continued to love him, and he hadn't given it a lot of thought past that. "That was a long time ago."

"Maybe the hell-raising, but you're still a law unto yourself, aren't you, brother? Luke Rutledge answers to no one except Luke Rutledge and the consequences be damned."

While Adam spoke, Luke focused on Olivia's expression as she worried her lower lip with her teeth. Adam had painted a damning, albeit fairly accurate, picture of Luke. Each word brush stroked doubt onto Olivia's face.

Luke remained seated, employing deliberate calm. "I'm my own man, Adam. I don't ask 'how high' when I'm told to jump, brother."

Adam reddened at the dig, but recovered quickly. He shook his head in disgust and turned his attention to

Olivia. "I understand he deceived you, darling. You thought you were with me. It's distasteful, but we'll get past it. It *was* just that once, when you thought he was me, wasn't it? You weren't *intimate* after you discovered Luke's true identity?"

Too bad Adam hadn't tracked down Spanish Inquisition attire. He was certainly playing the role.

It would be so easy for Olivia to save face. Technically, they hadn't physically consummated their relationship except for those first two times. Shame suffused her features. Luke felt her shame like a knife to the gut.

He jumped in before she could speak.

"No." He'd lie any day to erase her shame. He caught her eye, willing her to go along with his story.

Her expression condemned him for lying. In an effort to protect her from her own self-condemnation, he'd given credence to every charge Adam had leveled his way. How many times in the future—if they still had a future, would she feel shame because of something he'd done or said?

She turned away from Luke and up at Adam. "Yes. We were." She lowered her eyes. "Now you understand why I can't see you anymore."

A part of him died inside at her subtle, yet telling, distinction. She couldn't see Adam again because she'd betrayed him. Not because she cared for Luke.

"None of that matters, darling. It hurts that it happened, but it wasn't your fault. I know how Luke can be. He deceived you and then I'm sure he was relentless pursuing you." He cast a malevolent glance at Luke. "Regardless of how much damage he caused along the way, I forgive you. We'll put it behind us."

"But, Adam, I can't—"

"Yes, you can. Together we can. I had thought to do this under different circumstances but..."

An intense foreboding filled Luke as Adam dropped to one knee. Adam reached in his pocket and pulled out a velvet box. "Olivia, would you do me the honor of marrying me?"

OLIVIA REELED as if Adam had struck her. She'd anticipated scathing anger. She'd braced herself for denigration. Had he called her a whore, she wouldn't have been surprised. But this—Adam Hale Rutledge kneeling before her in a marriage proposal—rendered her speechless and more than a bit horrified.

"Put me out of my misery. Say yes. We can build a good life together, Olivia. We have the same interests. We want the same things. We'll work together to make Colther County a place our children will be proud of." An emerald-cut diamond mounted in a platinum setting dazzled her. But Adam offered up so much more than a beautiful ring. He dangled a glimpse of a family life she'd dreamed of, yearned for. Blood rushed to her head.

"I don't know what to say."

"Try no. A simple *no* would do," Luke drawled from the sofa.

Luke. For the space of a heartbeat, she'd forgotten about Luke. Stricken, she looked at him, his blue eyes pinning her with accusation. He knew.

Adam sneered over his shoulder at Luke. "Haven't you done enough harm already?" Adam faced Olivia and rose to his feet. Olivia had the inane thought that he looked absolutely ridiculous in his swashbuckler outfit with that patch sitting on his forehead like a third eye. "Olivia, I had hoped it wouldn't come to this. I wanted to spare you the ugly truth, but I had no idea he'd go so far. Luke has used you, my dear.''

Olivia sank back into the arms of the chair. She didn't like the sound of this. The implacable mask that was Luke's face knotted her stomach. "He's lying, Liv. He's the one that wants to use you.''

She looked from Adam to Luke and back again. Her heart racing, she clenched her hands into fists to still their trembling. "One of you explain, please.'' How could her voice remain so calm when she felt so frantic inside?

"Tell her the truth, Adam,'' Luke urged. His voice, low and calm, reminded her of a dangerous lull before an impending storm.

"Luke came to me a week or so ago with a proposition. He had the inside track on a proposed shopping center development—one of his construction contacts. Apparently your father is sitting on prime development property. He wanted me to use my influence with you and he'd handle your father. Of course I told him absolutely not.''

Time hung suspended as the bottom dropped out of her world. It made a sad sort of sense as to why a man like Luke would be interested in her. Much more sense than some mystical soul connection. "Why didn't you mention this to me?''

"Because I never thought he'd sink so low. I never thought he'd take it this far. I thought he'd approach your father and leave it at that. I suppose he wanted to double his chances by going through you.''

"He's lying, Liv. He's the one that came to me.'' Luke's voice rang calm and steady.

She wanted to believe him. She *ached* to believe him. "You could seduce me, sleep with me, yet you couldn't tell me Adam was using me? You didn't think I needed to know?" A shattering heart and crumbling self-esteem tended to make her testy.

"I didn't think you'd believe me." Luke shrugged, his face tight with anger at her challenge. "Much like right now."

Like a clip from a bad movie, she recalled Luke urging her to let him take her to see Pops. Luke and Pops sitting on the front porch. Tendrils of doubt stole through her, wrapping around her heart.

"Call him, Olivia. Ask your father. Ask him if either one of us ever mentioned selling his land," Adam urged her.

"Liv, your heart already knows if you'll just listen to it."

"What can it hurt to call your father?" Adam argued.

In the chaos running through her mind, it seemed a reasonable solution.

Olivia hit the speaker on the phone and dialed the number. The ring echoed through the small room. *Please let him tell her that Luke had never mentioned selling the land.* "Pops? It's Olivia."

"Hey, Olivia. How's the new wing coming along?"

"Fine." Olivia cut to the chase. "Pops, has Adam ever mentioned you selling the farm?"

"Adam who?"

"Adam Rutledge. He came to the house with me once."

"Not that I recall."

She should have been relieved. She wasn't. "Did Luke mention anything about the farm when we were out the other day?"

"No. No, I don't reckon he did."

She sagged with relief, even though she was no closer to getting to the bottom of the matter.

"Not that day. He didn't mention it until he stopped by last night. Something about a plan to sell the farm and invest the money. I'm not quite sure. I'd had a touch of the Turkey—for medicinal purposes. My arthritis was acting up again. Told him I wasn't interested in any investments. Say…"

Pops continued to talk but Olivia didn't hear past the roaring in her ears, filling her head.

"Thanks, Pops," she interrupted. "I'll call you later." She pushed the button and disconnected the call.

"This is a setup, Liv. I went to warn your father. Bennett was drinking but I hoped some of what I said would get through to him." He offered a wry grimace. "Apparently the wrong part did. I know it looks bad, but you've got to listen to me, baby."

"Which is exactly why he seduced you," Adam jumped in. "He doesn't want you to think clearly. Think about it, darling. Luke has no scruples. He's the one that deceived you and seduced you. He's the one who admits he's a law unto himself. His rules are the only ones he adheres to. He's the one who takes what he wants, does as he pleases and to hell with everyone else."

His words held a painful, numbing logic.

"I'm sorry I didn't stop him sooner. Did he profess undying love for you?" The thinly veiled sneer in Adam's voice salted her wounds. "Ah, I can see by the look on your face he did. What do you think would've happened once he had what he wanted from you? I'll tell you. He'd have left you with nothing except a ruined reputation and a healthy dose of humiliation. He'd strip you of your respectability and think nothing of it, Olivia."

Every doubt she'd faced and overcome, charged at her in full battle armor, battering her psyche. All of it had been a lie? Not just his feelings but the shift in her self-concept?

Adam took her hand in his. He poised the diamond ring above her finger with his other hand. "Let me put this ring on your finger. Let me share my name with you."

Olivia felt as if she were pinned to the shore, helpless to move as an enormous wave gained momentum. On the verge of drowning, she looked to Luke in mute appeal, desperate for him to refute the case against him before the wave crashed over her head. *Convince me once again* she begged him mutely.

Luke's eyes—those brilliant, beautiful cerulean eyes that had sparkled with wit, devilment, appreciation and seduction—gazed back at her now, the flat eyes of a dead man. He shrugged. "The game's up. It's true. I'll leave now."

He stood, a cold smile etched against the hard line of his mouth. "Don't bother seeing me to the door. I know the way."

Although her mind screamed in protest, she sat without movement as he strode to the door.

He paused in the doorway. "Welcome to the family, Liv."

The front door clicked with the impact of a gunshot. Adam began to slide the ring onto her finger. Olivia pulled her hand away very, very carefully. She felt hollow and brittle, as if she were a shell made of glass in danger of shattering into a million pieces. "I can't—"

"Don't say anything." He pressed the ring into her palm and curled her fingers around it. "Keep it, and think about it."

"I don't need to—"

Adam held up his finger. "Shh. This has all been something of a shock to you. I don't want you to make any rash decisions. Take a week to think about it. Consider the life we could build together. I find Luke's methods deplorable, but, while you're thinking about things, consider I could pull some strings and perhaps find a buyer for your father's land. If I invested and managed the profits for him, he'd never have to worry about money again. Just a thought. Now, why don't you run and change and we can still make dinner?"

Olivia's stomach roiled at the very thought. "I need some time alone. Maybe tomorrow night." She and Luke probably wouldn't keep that date now, she thought on a rising tide of hysteria. She edged toward the front door, the smell of Adam's cologne and hair gel adding to her nausea.

Annoyance flashed across Adam's face. Olivia was far too numb to care. "Of course, darling. I'll call you tomorrow." He gentled her against the front door, sliding his soft lips against hers. A shudder shook her.

"Good night, Liv."

Only Luke called her that. She couldn't bear to hear it on Adam's lips. She pushed him away.

"Don't call me that." Her directive came out much sharper than she'd intended. Her lips felt brittle and tight as she tried to smile. "Sorry. I prefer Olivia. Good night, Adam."

The door had barely closed behind him before she raced down the hall. She didn't bother to turn on the light as she dropped to the cold tile floor. Hanging her head over the toilet, she retched.

13

"HOW ABOUT A BEER?" Dave slid into the scarred wooden booth across from Luke, his face a mottled shade of blue and red in the neon glow of Cecil's beer signs. "Cynthia tossed me out for a few hours. PMS. What the hell's wrong with you? That time of the month for Olivia too?"

In the last few hours, Luke had nursed too few beers and smoked one too many cigars. All without any interference, thanks to his general surliness. Now he found himself in the unusual mood to spill his guts.

So, he did. The whole miserable tale.

"Let me get this straight. You took the fall for your brother, a son-of-a-bitch in sheep's clothing if I ever met one, so that he could marry the woman you love? Why don't you put that beer down and we'll step outside so I can knock some sense into you? That's the damn dumbest thing I've ever heard."

"You don't understand Olivia."

"Yeah? Well, neither do you. She's a woman. We're men. We're not supposed to understand them."

Actually, it might be better if he didn't understand her so well. Then he wouldn't have seen how much she wanted what Adam could offer. He wouldn't have seen the doubt eating at her when Adam described how Luke embarrassed the family. Then he would've charged full-speed ahead and done what he'd always done. He'd have fought for her and taken what he wanted. And eventually she would've hated him for it.

"If you had seen her face when Adam was painting the picture of what their life would be like...for one instant... And as much as I hate to admit it, he's right about two things. First, he can give Olivia the one thing she craves that I can't—respectability. Second, I am a selfish bastard. I've never given much thought to how I affected other people's lives. Maybe it's time I did."

"So, now you're a regular Sydney Carton?" Dave clutched his baseball cap to his chest and assumed a dramatic pose. "'It's a far, far better thing that I do now than I have ever done before.'" He slammed the cap back on his head. "You know, it doesn't end well for Syd. He dies in the end."

And so would he, a little bit every day. Each time he saw her. Thought of her. He swallowed a mouthful of warm, flat beer.

Dave shook his head, still mystified. "Your brother's a jerk. What happens when he gets his land? I don't think it's gonna do much for Olivia in the respectability department when he ditches her."

Luke managed a grim smile. "I plan to have a little talk with Adam. There won't be any land deal. I've got dirt on Adam and the Colonel. Graft involving a state politico is a fairly big deal. The first time I see Olivia and she doesn't look happy as a clam in sand, I'll ruin them." In a heartbeat and without hesitation.

Dave lowered his voice and leaned across the booth. "Graft?"

Luke nodded. "It was too easy to find out. The Colonel's so damn arrogant, he considers himself untouchable and didn't cover his tracks very well."

"How will you know if they make Olivia's life a living hell?"

"I'm returning to the bosom of the family. I'll be there for Sunday dinners, holidays, weddings. And I'll know." In the end, it was the only way to give her what she wanted.

"You've got it all figured out, don't you, big guy? Did it ever occur to you that Olivia deserves to make her own decisions?"

"She did. You weren't there. You didn't see her face."

"With all the correct facts."

Luke passed a weary hand over his bristled jaw. "I saw her. She struggled and she tried, but she's never going to get past measuring herself against the world's public opinion. And it'd only be a matter of time before I became an embarrassment."

Dave snorted.

"Trust me, it's better this way."

"I think you're one can shy of a six-pack." Dave sighed in resignation. "But I know that look and I'm not changing your mind, am I?"

"Nope. From now on, Olivia's like a sister to me." The words threatened to choke him. Maybe he was one can shy of a six-pack.

"So, YOU'RE SURE you don't want to marry Adam?" Tammy twisted around to eye Olivia from a counter stool. "You know it's not every day that a Cooper has the chance to marry a high and mighty Rutledge. Adam seems much more your type than Luke."

"Luke's not even a remote possibility." Olivia pasted on a smile. Neither was Adam. She'd taken his week and stretched it to two and then three. Each week she turned him down. Each week he told her to take more time while he painted a rosy picture of the two of them as Colther County's leading couple.

And every day she saw Luke's surreptitious glance at her ring finger and the flicker of relief and frustration her naked finger elicited. Every day they treated each other with polite professionalism, pretending the attraction that still pulsed between them didn't exist. Olivia despised herself that she could still ache for the touch of a man who'd humiliated her, betrayed her. One or two more days and the library expansion would be finished. Luke would be gone. And she'd have her life back. It couldn't come soon enough.

"I still can't see Luke trying to get your father's land. It doesn't seem like his style," Beth said, skimming through a baby magazine.

Olivia winced. She'd asked Beth to keep that particularly humiliating detail private, but her newfound pregnancy seemed to affect her memory.

Beth looked up from a glossy diaper ad. "Oops."

Tammy looked across the island from Beth to Olivia. Tammy had spent more and more time with Olivia in the last several weeks, their relationship shifting and growing. Had Olivia changed or had Tammy? Or was it a new understanding and acceptance for each other and their flaws that precipitated the change? Olivia wasn't sure, but it was nice to have found her sister.

"Luke told Pops Adam wanted his land. He told him Adam would offer to buy the land and invest the money for him. Luke said he was just giving him a heads-up. Pops said he'd never sell and that was that."

Olivia's legs refused to support her. She dropped to the stool. "How...when..."

"A couple of weeks ago when I was over at Pops's one night. I didn't bother to come out because I was in the middle of giving myself a pedicure and you'd already told me Luke was off-limits. Well, at the time he was."

Beth rubbed her pooching belly. "I told you Luke wouldn't do something like that."

"Yeah. I could've told you too, if someone had just asked," Tammy seconded.

"But why would he let me think..." A wave of nausea rolled over her and she stifled a gag. "All these years, I've resented having to prove myself past the label people gave me. Then I did the same thing to Luke. I ran with Adam's pillar-of-the-community label and Luke's bad-boy reputation." Luke had told her once that everyone wore a mask. Time and again, he'd shown her the real man he was, but she'd been too blinded by her own rigidity and insecurity to believe in him.

"You don't happen to have any ice cream in your freezer, do you?" Beth nibbled on a cracker. "Adam's a creep. I've been so afraid you were going to change your mind about his proposal."

Olivia sat immobilized. "I'm not sure."

Beth scowled. "How many times do I have to tell you he's a creep?"

"I'm sure about that. It's the ice cream—"

"I'll check." Tammy opened the freezer and brandished a carton of fudge ripple. "Olivia, you want a bowl too?"

Maybe a little ice cream would quell her queasiness. "Sure."

Tammy pulled out three bowls and rooted through the drawer for a scoop.

"So, Luke tells you he loves you but then he backs off and leaves the door open for Adam." Beth shook her head.

"Men." Tammy rolled her eyes as she handed Beth a

bowl of ice cream. "You can't live with 'em, and you can't shoot 'em."

"This doesn't make a bit of sense now. Luke isn't a backing off kind of guy. It only made sense if he was using you."

Tammy plopped down a small mountain of fudge ripple in front of her. Another piece of the puzzle fell into place. "It makes sense if you know Luke." And she did. He'd urged her to listen to her heart. He'd offered her his love and she'd thrown it back in his face with that one phone call to Pops. Adam hadn't offered her love. Adam had offered her the Cleaver ideal promoted by June, Wally and the Beave, and Luke had pushed her toward it.

Olivia pushed her ice cream to the middle of the island. "I can't eat that. I can barely look at it." She lived in a perpetual state of queasiness these days. She put it down to restless nights haunted by Luke and the general debacle her life had become.

Beth and Tammy exchanged a look. Tammy shook her head. "I think this is bad timing."

"There's no good timing," Beth argued. "You're her sister."

What were they going on about, now?

"You're her best friend," Tammy countered. "Okay, Chicken Little, I'll ask." Tammy turned to Olivia and shoved her hair behind her ear. "Well, you see...it's this way..." She waved her acrylics in the air. "We've been talking...have you considered..."

Beth snorted and broke in, "For sweet Pete's sake, I'll ask her." She directed herself to Olivia. "Is there any chance you might be pregnant?"

"Pregnant?" She pointed to Beth's stomach. "Like that?"

"Like this." Beth patted herself. "*This* is the only pregnant I know." She paused. "Just like there's only one way to get pregnant. Did you use anything?"

"Condoms." That was only once. That time against the door.... The phone sex didn't count. It was pretty near impossible to get pregnant over a phone.

Beth grabbed for her ice-cream bowl. "Do you mind?"

"Help yourself." Olivia waved the bowl away. One time without protection. She couldn't be pregnant. Could she? Unfortunately, she knew the answer to that question.

"I had a friend, once, who got pregnant using condoms." Beth gestured with her spoon. "You hear about the rubber breaking and everything but she swore that never happened. Must've just been a pinprick in the tip—no pun intended."

Olivia's stomach lurched.

Tammy scowled at Beth. "You must be getting a brain freeze or something from eating that so fast." She turned to Olivia. "Are you late?"

Dazed, Olivia checked the refrigerator calendar and did some quick calculations. She held on to the counter edge.

"A week. I'm a week late."

"Ohmigod. Ohmigod. Nobody panic. It's not good for the baby." Beth placed a protective hand over her stomach. "My baby that is. We don't know yet if you have a baby."

Tammy snapped her fingers—not an easy task given the length of her nails. "Put a sock in it, Beth, and get those hormones in control." Tammy turned to Olivia. "Queasy stomach?" Olivia nodded. "Tired?" Affirmative. "A week late?" Yes, again. "Sweet mother of pearl. Do you know whose it is?"

Heat slow-crawled up her face. The moment had come when her sister, who had single-handedly provided a surfeit of gossip, wanted to know if she, Olivia, had a clue as to her potential baby's father. "Of course I do. I haven't slept with Adam."

"That's a good one." Tammy chortled and then stopped when she realized she was the only one laughing. "But, you dated him."

"It never came up."

Beth started to speak, thought better of it and shoved in a spoonful of fudge ripple into her mouth instead.

"Whew. So, we know for sure it's Luke's baby." Tammy swiped her brow in an exaggerated gesture of relief.

"We don't know for sure if it's anybody's baby, because we don't know for sure whether I'm pregnant." Shock warred with exasperation. And she was beginning to believe it might be true. There was one opportunity and all the symptoms were there.

"If you were pregnant with Luke's baby and had married Adam, would the baby call Luke 'daddy' or 'uncle'?"

Olivia shuddered at Beth's question.

Tammy rolled her eyes. "Beth, shut up."

"There's only one way to tell. You're gonna have to pee on the stick." Beth didn't shut up.

Olivia sat in a daze, not quite getting it. She was still stuck on the daddy versus uncle dilemma. "Pee on a stick?"

"You know, a home pregnancy test. But you really need to take it in the morning when your urine's concentrated." Apparently her sister was no stranger to home pregnancy testing. "You would be a shoo-in for Jerry.

You could have both Luke and Adam on there to tell them. There was an episode just last week—"

Olivia felt close to fainting.

Beth interrupted Tammy. "If you do not shut up, I'm going to be forced to choke the life out of you."

"I never knew pregnant women were so mean...."

"That's it. Come here." Beth leaned across the island. "Let me get my hands on you...."

"Stop it, you two." Olivia buried her face in her hands. "My life has morphed into a soap opera."

"Yeah, it kind of has, hasn't it?" Tammy agreed good-naturedly.

"Go ahead and say something." Olivia thought back to all the times she hadn't managed to stem her self-righteous disapproval over Tammy.

Tammy frowned, puzzled. "Congratulations? Listen, why don't I run up to Snook's Drug Store and pick up one of those pregnancy tests for you. It'll take about two seconds for news like that to travel around town and my reputation's already shot to hell."

There wasn't any self-righteous condemnation from Tammy. No, woe is me, I'll be so embarrassed by my sister.

Olivia dammed back an onslaught of tears. "You would do that for me? Open yourself up to that kind of gossip?"

"Of course I would. What does it matter to me what those people say? If they're my friends they either don't care or don't talk, and as for the rest of them, to hell with them." Tammy caught herself. "But I know that stuff is a big deal to you."

The final piece of the puzzle, the elusive key she'd been missing all her life, appeared before her without any flash of lightning or clap of thunder to mark the moment. She hadn't spent a lifetime trying to prove to everyone else that she was worthy. All the machinations, all the approval had been sought to prove her worth not to others, but to herself. Living with the passion Luke provoked wouldn't diminish her, it would enrich her life. For the first time in a lifetime, Olivia acknowledged who she was and where she came from without an undercurrent of shame.

"I don't care what anyone says, you *are* a nice girl," Beth teased Tammy with a grin.

"Well, for God's sake, don't tell anyone. What the town gossips don't know won't hurt them." Tammy returned the smirk as she snatched up her purse. "I'll be back from Snook's in no time."

Olivia stiffened her spine and sucked up her tears. "Sit back down, Tammy. I appreciate the offer, and especially the sentiment, but I got myself in this predicament so I'll buy my own pregnancy test." She sat up taller. "If they're my friends they either don't care or won't talk, right?"

DAWN SEEPED INTO the room, bit by bit. It crept on silent feet past the edge of the curtain, across hardwood flooring and smooth white ceiling. Olivia turned her cheek to the sueded silk beneath her head—her personal horsehair shirt. She couldn't bear to get rid of them, but each time she touched them, slept on them, they flayed her with bittersweet memories of Luke.

She could get up now and go into her bathroom. Both kits were readied beside the sink. Two different brands from two separate manufacturers. Insurance. No second-guessing.

Either way, her life would never be the same. How absolutely befitting that the girl from the wrong side of the tracks had finally lived down to everyone's expectations. She grinned all over herself. Not just a little drunken episode in the town square that landed her a night in jail. Not a proclivity for a flavor of the year when it came to husbands. No. She'd managed the granddaddy of them all. Unmarried and pregnant, her baby's father a rebel.

She could already hear the whispers. Feel the stares. The sudden break in conversation when she walked into a room. And it was okay.

Marching into Snook's and buying those home pregnancy tests had been an act of deliberation and liberation. She, Olivia Cooper, was a real person. Anything short of sainthood didn't make her white trash.

She wasn't a fool. She might have to fight for her job and her position on the literacy council. But she would fight and she'd win because she'd had a tremendous positive impact on the library and the literacy council. She had skills, maturity and a nice little nest egg on her side.

She also had Beth and oddly enough she knew she could count on Tammy. And Luke? Where did Luke fit in? She would welcome him into her and their child's life.

And if there was no baby? If she tested negative? Essentially the same game plan, minus the baby element. She would move heaven and earth to convince Luke she was ready to live her own life according to her own standards and that included him, if he'd still have her.

Olivia pushed back the cocooning warmth of silk sheets and down comforter. It was cold in the house and trepidation set her heart racing. Nonetheless she swung her legs over the side of the bed and stood firmly on her own two feet.

Beth had once consulted a psychic who'd predicted her future by reading tea leaves. Olivia just had to read two sticks to discern hers.

LUKE PAUSED outside the kitchen at River Oaks and checked his boots, an acute sense of déjà vu washing over him. This is how it had all started four weeks ago.

An overwhelming array of finger foods covered every counter surface and the old-fashioned sideboard. "Big event tonight?"

Ruth harrumphed. "Did you check your boots?"

"Yes, ma'am. Clean as a whistle."

Ruth slipped an oversized spatula beneath a row of fat sausage balls. Sausage, cheese and the sharp bite of cayenne scented the air.

Ruth plucked one off her spatula and placed it on a saucer in front of him. "Why don't you sample that for me?" She shot him a look from beneath her white brows. "Cocktail party. Your brother keeps dropping hints he's going to announce his engagement."

"Here's to the happy couple." Luke bit into the warm sausage ball. It tasted like sawdust in his mouth.

"I still can't quite believe it. Adam and Olivia. At one time I'd thought...never mind."

"What?"

"I'd thought that maybe you and Olivia..."

He ached at the thought. "Why would you think that?"

"Just a crazy notion, I suppose."

"Olivia deserves better than someone like me. Someone who can give her the things she needs." His money more than matched Adam's, but he knew that had never been important to Olivia. He'd never have Adam's social standing and acceptance.

"Adam isn't near the man you are. In my book, he doesn't come close to deserving Olivia." Ruth brandished her spatula like a weapon. "Sit down and you listen up." Ruth's voice brooked no argument. Luke folded himself onto a ladder-back chair. "Don't you ever let me hear you say that again. You are one of the finest men I know. It's true you've always had a streak of the wild in you and you've given your mama more than a few gray hairs, but you're a man of integrity. Don't you ever forget that."

"But Adam—"

"Adam!" Ruth whacked the end off a bunch of celery. "Olivia needs someone to show her how to have fun. That gal needs to lighten up."

"Adam's perfect for Olivia. Respectable. Upstanding. Just what she needs."

"That's a bunch of hogwash and you know it. She needs what everybody needs—someone to love and respect her for who she is, not who she pretends to be. Now, if you're scared to stand up to the task, let's hope Adam does." *Whack. Whack. Whack.* More celery neatly stacked on a plate.

"Scared?" Surely he hadn't heard her correctly.

"That's what I said. If you're afraid you might let her down, then step aside. No need to worry about being a husband and father when you can sit back and be a brother-in-law and an uncle."

Luke barely breathed. "Uncle? Did you say uncle?"

"You know I don't gossip. But seeing as you're practically family...Lois Shrimpton was in Snook's last night. Her husband has a terrible time with the gout and she'd stopped by to pick up his medicine." Luke forced himself not to yell that he didn't give a rat's ass about Ed Shrimpton's gout. "Anyway, she was right behind Olivia in the checkout line. Olivia bought two home pregnancy tests, a quart of vanilla ice cream and a jar of pickles."

His Olivia? Uh, he meant Adam's Olivia. "Maybe Lois was mistaken. Doesn't she wear glasses?"

"Yep. She's having cataract surgery next month. But she knows for sure because the checkout girl had to call for a price check."

Despite the turmoil churning his gut, Luke had to laugh. "I bet Olivia almost went through the floor."

"Actually she said Olivia seemed chipper, downright excited." Ruth piped cream cheese down the middle of a celery stalk. "So, how do you feel about being an uncle?"

If there was a baby, there was only one father. Just last week, Adam had whined that Olivia wouldn't sleep with him. "I don't see how—"

"Obviously Olivia had relations. Abstinence is the only surefire way to keep from making babies that I know of, so don't tell me you don't know how this happened." *He did know how it happened. That one time against the door.* Ruth punctuated her words, jabbing in his direction. He wished she'd put that butcher knife down. "Now, like I was saying before, how do you feel about being an uncle?"

Somehow, in the face of potential fatherhood, his sacrifice didn't seem as noble as it did...well, stupid.

"I have no idea." He paused, weighing his options. The way he saw it, there was only one. "But I'm real excited about being a daddy."

14

OLIVIA STOOD next to her car and absorbed the splendor that was River Oaks. Soaring columns, graceful arched windows, immaculate formal gardens all bespoke generations of privilege.

She glanced at the ring on her finger as she approached the house via the front walk. It was much more than just a ring. It was a ticket, a passport to a different way of life. It was the key that gained her admission to River Oaks and its world.

She mounted the front steps. It was time for her to return the key. For weeks, she'd said no, but held on to it. She'd known all along she couldn't marry Adam, but she'd held on to the key. The key and all it represented no longer held any appeal. She was ready to move on with her life.

She knocked on the front door. Almost immediately Ralphie, decked out in his psuedobutler's uniform, admitted her. Once again, the grandeur of River Oaks took her breath. Beyond the foyer, a dozen people moved in and out of rooms, carrying tables, flowers and all the accoutrements for an elegant party.

"Olivia! If you aren't the cat's meow. Heard there might be an engagement." He winked at her. "You're moving up in the world, girl."

"Ralphie, you're a fool, but it really isn't your fault. Your side of the family can be that way." He grinned good-naturedly at her ribbing. "Do you know where Adam is?"

"I think he's in the library. Hold on. I'll find him for you."

She waited on Ralphie to return with Adam, watching all the people scurry about.

Ralphie reappeared with Adam in tow.

"Olivia, darling, I hope you're here with good news." Adam didn't speak to her these days without a strain in his voice. He stopped abruptly, really looking at her. "What in the name of heaven have you done to your hair?"

Well, good grief. That was a telling response. "I highlighted it. I decided it was time for a change. How do you like this shade of red?" She personally loved it.

Adam swallowed hard. "It's, uh, very...bright."

The house was overrun with people and they needed privacy. Even though she was a new woman, she still drew the line at totally making a spectacle of herself. "Could we talk out on the terrace?"

"Uh, sure. It's this way." He led her down the hallway, his hand resting on the small of her back. "You certainly look happy today. Which leads me to believe you're about to make me very happy as well."

She couldn't vouch for him. "I'm very happy, Adam. I'm happier today than I've ever been."

LUKE LEFT THE STABLES, having fulfilled his duty by admiring his mother's latest Arabian acquisition. He started down the path to the river, skirting the terrace. Dammit, where was Olivia? After talking to Ruth, he'd tried the library, her house, crazy Beth's house, her father's house. No Olivia. He'd been too damned keyed up to sit around and wait on her to show up at her house.

He stopped beneath a broad-armed oak to light a cigar, the suggestion of a breeze cool against his neck. The door leading from the ballroom opened and Luke stilled his lighter. Olivia and Adam stepped out.

"I have something to tell you," she said to Adam.

At least he thought it was Olivia. She walked like Olivia. She talked like Olivia. But this woman had glorious, bright red hair.

She walked over and sat on the low, stone balustrade. Luke soaked up her presence. If possible, she'd grown even more beautiful. Luke stood beneath the moss-draped tree, transfixed.

"There's no easy way to say this, Adam. So, let me just be blunt." She pulled the ring out of her pocket and held it out to Adam. "There's no point in me holding on to this. I'm not going to marry you. I could hold on to it for a lifetime and I still wouldn't change my mind."

Relief flooded Luke. Those were some of the sweetest words he'd ever heard. Now he wouldn't need to coerce her into giving up Adam.

The level of dismay on Adam's face verged on comic. Except no one was laughing. "But you have to marry me."

Olivia shook her head. "No. I don't have to and I'm not." She placed the ring on the stone wall.

"But why not? There has to be a reason."

Luke gripped the rough bark of the tree. There was only one thing he knew that would induce Olivia to give Adam back his ring. She'd never marry his brother if she was pregnant with Luke's child.

"It's simple really. I don't love you." And what about the baby?

"You don't have to love me." Sweat glistened on Adam's brow. He'd taken Luke's threat to expose him very seriously, as he should have. "That will come. It'll grow. We have a good, solid foundation." Adam threw his arm wide in an encompassing gesture. "All of this can be yours. Put the ring back on and it's yours."

The wind rustled through the trees, ruffling the Spanish moss that hung lacelike from the branches. Olivia's scent drifted past him.

"I don't expect you to ever understand this, but I don't want it."

"You don't mean that. You don't know what you're saying. I'll buy you a new car for our engagement. Your choice. Mercedes? Cadillac? Lexus? BMW? Range Rover? We'll go tomorrow and pick one out."

"How about a Harley? Would you buy me a Harley? Would you ride with me?"

She wasn't riding a damn motorcycle if she was pregnant.

"What about a Jaguar? A Porsche?" Olivia shook her head. Adam swallowed hard. "Okay, uh, I suppose it's a Harley, if that's what you want. But do I have to ride it as well?"

Olivia laughed. "You don't have to ride it and I don't expect you to buy it. I'm just teasing you, Adam."

Adam stood stiffly in front of her. "This is not a laughing matter."

"No, you're right. It's not." Olivia sobered appropriately.

"Why are you doing this, Olivia?"

"I was a fool a couple of weeks ago. Actually, I've been a fool for a long time." Olivia spoke softly but her voice carried clearly across the terrace. "Luke never wanted my father's land."

Adam's right eye twitched. "How do you know he doesn't want your father's land?"

"Because the truth found you out and I know Luke. I finally stopped being so damned frightened and listened to my heart. I'm ashamed that I listened to you that night at my house. I don't know if Luke will have me." Wry deprecation marked her tone. "I don't even know if he wants me. What I do know is I deserve better than settling for second best. And make no mistake about it Adam, you are second best."

She'd tried to be true to herself once before. It had damn near killed him when she couldn't.

"There's no need to be insulting." Adam feigned an injured air.

"I didn't notice you holding back that day. And it's the truth." Olivia heaped insult on injury.

"Fine. But you've got to tell him this, Olivia. He's got to hear it from you. He'll never believe me."

Luke stepped out of the moss-draped shadows, into the sunlight. "You're right, I probably wouldn't have believed *you*, Adam."

"Luke?"

"Luke!" Olivia took a step toward him, then stopped in surprise. "You cut your hair."

Luke ran his hand along his bare neck. "Yeah, I guess I did. Thought it was time to look a little more respectable. You colored yours."

She lifted a hand to her red highlights. "My personal version of the scarlet letter." She glanced up at him, prim and proper in her neat navy suit, her gray eyes smoldering with promise behind those tortoiseshell glasses. He recognized that look. It was a closed front door, silk sheets, a kitchen counter, the luster of pearls against bare skin. His body tightened in familiar response. "A gentleman wouldn't eavesdrop."

"It's a good thing I'm not one." He cupped her jaw in his callused palm. A tremor shook him—it had been sheer hell to see her and not touch her for the last several weeks.

"Cut it out you two. You heard her, didn't you, Luke? It's not my fault she's not happy."

Luke ignored Adam. "Is there something you want to tell me, Liv?"

She placed her hands on his shoulders and stared into his eyes. "I love you."

Happiness so intense it damn near took his breath flooded him. He stroked the softness of her neck. She trembled at his touch. "I know."

"That's right. You heard." Her tongue teased the tip of his finger.

It felt so good—the wet tip of her tongue. If he didn't ask her soon, he'd forget what it was he meant to say. "Is there anything else? Are you...are we...is there going to be—"

"Are you asking me if I'm pregnant?" She entwined her fingers with his, and held their linked hands between them.

Luke could barely breathe. "Yes. That's what I'm asking. Are we having a baby?"

"No. I'm not pregnant. Two tests. Both negative."

He'd been so sure she was, he couldn't quite believe she wasn't. "But what about the ice cream and pickles?"

"Pregnant? Why didn't you just tell me that's why you couldn't marry me instead of handing me that wad of second-best crap?"

Damn, he'd forgotten all about Adam.

"I picked them up for Beth. I've just been so miserable

without you, my whole body's off-kilter." She turned to Adam. "And you're right. You're not second best. I think you're somewhere much further down the line."

Adam snatched up the ring. "The two of you definitely deserve one another." He huffed across the terrace and stalked into the house.

"He's right you know, we deserve one another." She linked her hands behind his head, teasing her fingers against his bare neck. "Did you only speak up because you thought I was pregnant?"

He splayed his hands against the curve of her hips. Fire licked through his veins. Liv had finally stopped fighting the woman she was. "Nah. Sooner or later Dave or Ruth or the both of them would've knocked some sense into me."

"So, how do you feel about children?" She curled her fingers up into his hair.

Hmm. Her hands felt so good on him. How did he feel about what? Oh, yeah. Kids. "I like them. I think we should spend the next several years working on them. Right after we go pick out that Harley. Or you could just ride on mine."

"Hmm. It's always so stimulating when I ride with you. Luke? Why did you let me think you'd used me? Why did you stand by and watch me choose Adam?"

"I was suffering from a Sydney Carton complex. Adam could offer you the one thing I couldn't. And I still can't—respectability. It takes more than a haircut."

Her lips curled in triumph and satisfaction. "I knew it. You are a crazy, misguided man, and I love you to distraction. What changed your mind?"

"You know, things didn't turn out well for Syd." There was no law that said he had to be original. "And I like to make my own rules. I can't offer you the Cleavers.

I can't promise you that things will always be good. What I can tell you is that I love you and I want to build a life with you." He reached in his pocket and pulled out the long velvet box he'd picked up at the jewelers less than two hours ago.

"You were so sure of me."

"I wasn't so sure of anything. Except I wasn't going to give you up without a fight." He traced the sensitive shell of her ear. "Even if it meant resorting once more to seduction." He traced the fullness of her lower lip with his thumb. "Pillage." She took his thumb into her mouth. "Plunder."

"Yes."

"Yes to what?"

"All of the above. I think you're definitely going to have to resort to piracy." Her tongue swirled around his joint. "Pillage." It teased against his tip. "Plunder."

"Good God, woman. Would you open the damn present before I die from an erection?"

Olivia released his thumb and lifted the lid on the box. A wood-carved miniature mask, polished to a rich hue, lay nestled in velvet, suspended from a fine gold chain.

"Luke, it's beautiful." She lifted it reverently from the box. "It's exquisite. Where did you ever find something so perfect?"

"I made it. I had the jewelers put it on the chain. You like it?"

"I don't hate it." She presented it for him to put on her.

Luke grinned like a kid in a candy store. "That's good."

"I don't just like it a little."

He fastened it around her neck and tugged her closer into his arms. "No?"

"I love it." She stood on tiptoe, her lips brushing his in tender promise.

Luke looked over Olivia's shoulder. Several pairs of eyes stared back from the ballroom windows.

"Uh, Liv?"

She reluctantly redirected her attention, "Yes?"

He indicated their audience. She turned. "People are going to talk."

"I suppose they will." She waved at the crowd and turned back to him. "How would you feel about a private treasure hunt?"

"I might be interested."

Her seductive smile mocked his understatement. "I could take you to this island I know."

In her kitchen. Luke swallowed hard. "Sounds promising."

She scraped her fingernail against his throat and his body shuddered as if she'd stroked him lower. Her breath stirred against his mouth. "The only jewels there are pearls. If you're interested, I'd love to show them to you." Her gray eyes glittered behind her glasses.

He laughed softly at her sly teasing, despite the fierce hunger she stirred in him. He pulled her curves against the hard lines of his body. "There's *almost* nothing I like better than a treasure hunt."

She arched against him intimately. "Be sure to bring your sword with you."

And then Lady Olivia proceeded to kiss him just this side of senseless.

Princes...Princesses...
London Castles...New York Mansions...
To live the life of a royal!

In 2002, Harlequin Books lets you escape to a world of royalty with these royally themed titles:

Temptation:
January 2002—*A Prince of a Guy* (#861)
February 2002—*A Noble Pursuit* (#865)

American Romance:
The Carradignes: American Royalty (Editorially linked series)
March 2002—*The Improperly Pregnant Princess* (#913)
April 2002—*The Unlawfully Wedded Princess* (#917)
May 2002—*The Simply Scandalous Princess* (#921)
November 2002—*The Inconveniently Engaged Prince* (#945)

Intrigue:
The Carradignes: A Royal Mystery (Editorially linked series)
June 2002—*The Duke's Covert Mission* (#666)

Chicago Confidential
September 2002—*Prince Under Cover* (#678)

The Crown Affair
October 2002—*Royal Target* (#682)
November 2002—*Royal Ransom* (#686)
December 2002—*Royal Pursuit* (#690)

Harlequin Romance:
June 2002—*His Majesty's Marriage* (#3703)
July 2002—*The Prince's Proposal* (#3709)

Harlequin Presents:
August 2002—*Society Weddings* (#2268)
September 2002—*The Prince's Pleasure* (#2274)

Duets:
September 2002—*Once Upon a Tiara/Henry Ever After* (#83)
October 2002—*Natalia's Story/Andrea's Story* (#85)

Celebrate a year of royalty with Harlequin Books!

Available at your favorite retail outlet.

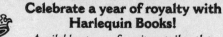

HARLEQUIN®

Makes any time special ®

Visit us at www.eHarlequin.com

HSROY02

Who was she really?

Where Memories Lie

GAYLE
WILSON

AMANDA
STEVENS

Two full-length novels of enticing, romantic suspense—by
two favorite authors.

They don't remember their names or lives, but the two
heroines in these two fascinating novels do know one thing:
they are women of passion. Can love help bring back the
memories they've lost?

Look for WHERE MEMORIES LIE in July 2002—
wherever books are sold.